The EDUCATION of HAILEY KENDRICK

Also by EILEEN COOK

What Would Emma Do?
Getting Revenge on Lauren Wood

The EDUCATION *of* HAILEY KENDRICK

EILEEN COOK

SIMON PULSE
New York London Toronto Sydney

This book is a work of fiction. Any references to historical events, real people, or real locales are used fictitiously. Other names, characters, places, and incidents are the product of the author's imagination, and any resemblance to actual events or locales or persons, living or dead, is entirely coincidental.

SIMON PULSE
An imprint of Simon & Schuster Children's Publishing Division
1230 Avenue of the Americas, New York, NY 10020
First Simon Pulse hardcover edition January 2011
Copyright © 2011 by Eileen Cook
All rights reserved, including the right of reproduction
in whole or in part in any form.
SIMON PULSE logo and colophon are registered trademarks
of Simon & Schuster, Inc.
For information about special discounts for bulk purchases,
please contact Simon & Schuster Special Sales at 1-866-506-1949
or business@simonandschuster.com.
The Simon & Schuster Speakers Bureau can bring authors to your live event.
For more information or to book an event contact the Simon & Schuster Speakers
Bureau at 1-866-248-3049 or visit our website at www.simonspeakers.com.
The text of this book was set in Adobe Garamond.
Manufactured in the United States of America
2 4 6 8 10 9 7 5 3 1
Library of Congress Cataloging-in-Publication Data
Cook, Eileen.
The education of Hailey Kendrick / by Eileen Cook. —
1st Simon Pulse hardcover ed.
p. cm.
Summary: Dating a popular boy and adhering to every rule ever written,
a high school senior at an elite Vermont boarding school begins to shed
her good-girl identity after an angry incident with her distant father.
ISBN 978-1-4424-1325-2
[1. Self-perception—Fiction. 2. Dating (Social customs)—Fiction.
3. Boarding schools—Fiction. 4. Schools—Fiction.] I. Title.
PZ7.C76955Ed 2011
[Fic]—dc22
2010025608
ISBN 978-1-4424-1330-6 (eBook)

TO MOM AND DAD,
WHO TAUGHT ME
TO LOVE BOOKS

1

There was a matter of life and death to deal with, and instead we were wasting our time discussing Mandy Gallaway's crotch. I kept a neutral smile plastered on my face, but my foot bobbed up and down impatiently. More people have seen Mandy Gallaway's naked crotch than saw last year's Super Bowl. The girl's incapable of getting out of a car without flashing the sixty zillion paparazzi that follow her around. The concept of knees together and underwear on isn't that complicated, which leaves me to believe she likes the sensation of flashbulbs lighting up where the sun isn't supposed to shine.

Given that her crotch had been photographed more than most supermodels, I failed to see why one online leaked picture of her standing in her gym shorts and a sports bra was causing this much drama. The situation certainly didn't call for the public flogging and stoning the student body was advocating.

All the crowd was missing were some pitchforks and torches, and we could have stormed the town. On the upside, at least people had shown up for our student government meeting, for a change.

The Evesham student body usually had more important things to care about, like planning their next vacation to a private island near the Bahamas, or deciding between another Coach or Louis Vuitton bag. Most of the time the only people who came to our meetings were those of us on the board.

It wasn't clear what had really happened, but the theory was that a female security guard had snapped the photo of the half-dressed Mandy in the locker room and had sold it to the tabloids. A few people had seen a guard doing her rounds of the gym, and she'd had her cell phone out. Given who attends Evesham, paparazzi is a common problem, but before this incident they'd tended to hang outside the school gates. No one had ever had a picture leaked from inside. This was officially big news on campus.

"We should send her to prison for violating Mandy's privacy," Garrett said. His dad is a U.S. Senator; you would think he would have a better idea of how the system works.

"We're a student government association," I pointed out. "We don't actually have the power to sentence anyone to jail time." I straightened the nameplate on the desk in front of me: HAILEY KENDRICK—VICE PRESIDENT. I managed to avoid pointing out that we barely had the authority to hold a bake sale.

"Whatever. I want her fired," Mandy said. "Like, today." She crossed her arms and stuck her chin up into the air.

"We can't have her fired, either. The school employees all belong to a union. The whole thing is outside of the student government domain. It's up to the administration." I considered pulling the copy of the employee union agreement out of my file, but I was pretty sure no one was interested in the details of due process. It wasn't exactly a big pro-union crowd. I didn't know why we bothered to have this issue on the agenda at all, except for the fact that everyone wanted to talk about it.

"Really?" Mandy raised one perfectly plucked eyebrow. "If the administration isn't interested in what students think, maybe I should have my parents give them a call."

Mandy's parents had more money than most countries. I was pretty sure they could buy up some small ones—Luxembourg or the Philippines, for example—without even breaking the monthly budget. Her great-grandparents had owned several oil and gas companies and hung out with people like the Vanderbilts. If her parents called the school administration and said jump, people there would start leaping around before even bothering to ask how high.

I looked at the clock. We were going to run out of time. In addition to tackling the safety issue I had hoped to discuss, the council meeting was supposed to be focused on choosing between the two possible themes for our spring formal dance. Any talk of Southern Nights or Old Hollywood had gone out the door when the news about the picture had spread across campus. It was standing room only in the classroom we used for our meetings. No one wanted to miss any hot dirt.

"It totally grosses me out that that dyke took my picture." Mandy made a face like she had just bitten into month-old cottage cheese.

"Careful," Joel said. As the president of the student council, he was always sure to enforce the "respect and dignity" clause in the student handbook. "Her sexual orientation isn't an issue here."

"God, it's not a gay thing. I have tons of family friends who are gay," Mandy said. "'Dyke' is just a description."

It was classic Mandy to make a distinction between okay gay people (those who design houses or clothing, work in Hollywood, or write for the *New Yorker*) and not okay gay people (women who wear flannel shirts from Walmart.) The real issue wasn't the fact that the security guard might be gay, it was that she had a cheap haircut and unshaven legs, and had made a few thousand dollars selling an unflattering photo of Mandy. Even the haircut, flannel, and legs might have been forgiven if the photo hadn't made Mandy's thighs look a bit chunky.

Joel clapped his hands together to get everyone's attention. "Hailey is right. This issue doesn't fall under student government business." The crowd in the room started to grumble and protest, and Joel held up one hand. "That doesn't mean we can't make it our business."

A cheer went up from the group. Joel was a natural politi-

4

cian. I was certain he would be president of the United States someday. He had written to every living former president and asked them for advice on leadership. He kept the letters he got back in a binder in his room. President Clinton had sent him at least four. Not many people can list a president of the United States as a pen pal.

Joel stood so the people at the back could see him. "Privacy and the ability of everyone to feel safe here at Evesham is critical, and is a value this government is willing to fight to uphold. This isn't just a boarding school; it's our home away from home. We go to school here. We live here. We need to feel safe here. I motion that the council write a formal letter to the school administration indicating our concerns and demanding that action be taken. All in favor?"

There was a chorus of cheers and whoops from the crowd. Joel looked at me, and I could see the corner of his mouth twitching as he fought off a smile. He knew we could write all the letters we wanted and the school administration would still do whatever they wanted. However, he'd convinced everyone that he was practically Superman standing up for truth, justice, and the American way. Saving the rich and privileged from unflattering photos. I rolled my eyes at him and pressed my mouth together to avoid smiling. If I gave him any encouragement, there was no telling what he would come up with next.

"We have to have someone second the motion and put it to a vote," I said.

"Why? Is there some rule?" Garret said. I wanted to smack the smirk right off his face. As a matter of fact, there was a rule. If he wanted the Save the Crotch letter, then there was going to be an official vote. I stared at him with a smile on my face and said nothing.

"I'll second the motion," a sophomore girl sitting on the floor said. Joel gave her one of his thousand-watt smiles. Her face flushed bright red, and she let out a high-pitched giggle.

"Great. Now we just need to get a count of all those in favor," Joel said, and called for a show of hands.

I heard a sound behind me, and I turned to see my boyfriend, Tristan, leaning in the doorway. I held up a finger to let him know it would only be a couple of minutes more. Not surprisingly, no one was opposed to the Save the Crotch letter, and it passed.

"We still need to decide on the theme for the dance," I said before Joel had a chance to dismiss the meeting.

"What theme do you want?" Tristan called from the doorway.

"I don't want to influence the vote," I said.

"I'm thinking you'd go for the Hollywood glamour option," Tristan said, cocking his head to the side as if he were picking up my brain waves.

"So, are you guessing or making a motion?" Joel asked.

Tristan flipped Joel off, and they both laughed. They'd been roommates since freshman year. As upperclassmen they'd qualified to each get their own room, but they still preferred to share. Tristan found it difficult to trust many people, and he always swore that Joel was more than his friend, that they were brothers. You could tell by looking at them they might be brothers of choice, but they weren't remotely related. Joel was tall and lanky. He always had to be in motion. I didn't have a single photo of Joel where his image wasn't partially blurred. Tristan was the opposite. He seemed unmovable. He was tall too, but broad. One of the first things that had attracted me to him was how solid he appeared. Tristan looked like he could stand straight during a hurricane.

"It's a motion, Mr. President," Tristan said with a slight bow.

"Anyone care to second?" Joel called out, and the room filled with hands raised to support Tristan. Joel was the politician, but Tristan was the charmer. It was almost unfair to have that much male charisma in one dorm room. "Great. Now a quick vote. All in favor?" The sea of hands raised again. "Anyone opposed?" He looked around the room, but no one was interested in going against Tristan. Joel looked over at me. "Looks like we have a dance theme. With our business finished, I call this meeting officially to an end."

Tristan stood next to me while everyone else streamed out of the room. Mandy paused long enough to lean into Joel, pressing her breasts against his chest (there was a running bet that they were fake, which is likely, because no one has breasts that size and that perky, unless they're filled with a space-age material) and thanking him for standing up for her. Her voice was slightly breathless, as if she were nearly overcome with gratitude. She was acting like he had carried her down twenty-two flights of stairs in a burning building. Both Joel and Tristan turned to watch her stroll out, her hips going back and forth like she was walking across the deck of a listing ship.

"Careful. Your eyes might fall out," I said.

Tristan looked away, then pulled me close to nuzzle my ear. "The girl can't hold a candle to you. She's all flash and glitter. It would be like dating a disco ball." He looked up at Joel. "You should ask her to the dance. She looks pretty grateful."

"Oh, so *I* can have the disco ball. Thanks, man. Your kindness knows no bounds."

"You need something a little flashy to keep your attention. You get distracted pretty easy. It's a good thing we're seniors, because you're running out of girls to date."

Joel punched Tristan in the arm, and they jostled around laughing.

"You can do better than Mandy," I said to Joel while I stuffed papers into my bag.

"I keep trying to convince you to run away with me, but you won't leave this ape," Joel said, ducking a headlock from Tristan. Joel darted across the room, hooting like a monkey. Very fourth grade.

"I'm glad we got the dance settled. I was afraid we weren't going to get to it, " I said.

"We can put the idea of securing the vending machines on next month's agenda," Joel said, raising his hand like he was taking a vow.

Tristan raised an eyebrow at Joel. "Vending machine safety?"

I rolled my eyes at both of them. I was used to being teased about my safety obsession. People could laugh all they wanted. The one thing I knew for sure was that the world was a dangerous and unpredictable place. Smart people do everything they can to eliminate risk. Did you know that more people are killed every year in falling vending machine accidents than in shark attacks? Our school had an entire wall of unsecured vending machines in the lobby of the gym. If someone were crushed to death trying to get a frosty can of Diet Coke, it wouldn't be my fault. I'd tried to raise the issue.

"Today's agenda sort of got hijacked. Nothing riles people up like a good scandal and a sense of righteous justice," Joel said.

"Do you think they'll fire the security guard?" I asked.

"They shouldn't. There isn't any real proof, and if she doesn't have any other disciplinary notes in her employment file, I'm willing to bet the union rules say they can't."

"They should." Tristan's voice turned serious. I wasn't surprised. Having parents with four Oscars between them meant you could have Steven Spielberg as your godfather, but never a moment of privacy. His ninth birthday had been ruined when a photographer had fallen out of a tree onto the pool deck while trying to get a picture of his parents. "You aren't taking her side, are you?" Tristan asked Joel.

"I'm not taking anyone's side. Just saying she doesn't deserve to be burned at the stake until we know what really happened." He looked over at Tristan. "You don't have to worry, dude. No one wants a picture of your ugly half-dressed ass."

"Except you," Tristan shot back. "I've seen how you look at me."

I rolled my eyes. "I'll let you guys have some special alone time. I'm supposed to meet up with Kelsie to work on our history project."

"Hang out with us. We're going to the café to get some ice cream. What sounds like more fun, ice cream or the Revolutionary War?" Tristan held on to my hand. He rubbed his thumb against the inside of my palm, a move that always gave me shivers. "Even George Washington would pick mint chocolate chip, and he had freedom on the line."

"George didn't have to worry about college applications," I pointed out, pulling my hand away before how he made me feel distracted me from homework. I was dedicated to getting good grades, but time with Tristan was never a bad thing. I kissed his cheek.

"Fine. Abandon us," Joel said, grabbing his stuff from the table. "I'm used to you snubbing me, but I'm not sure how he's going to handle it."

"I'm sure he can soldier on without me for a few hours."

"Despite the fact that you're breaking my heart, I still have amazing news for you," Tristan said.

"What?"

"I don't know if I'm going to tell you," he said, turning away. "I may be too devastated to talk now."

I smacked him across the shoulder. "Tell me."

"It's going to cost you a kiss," Tristan said.

I quickly kissed him.

"It's a way better secret than that," he said, leaning back against the table and crossing his arms.

I leaned in and he pulled me closer. He wound his hands into my hair and kissed me deeply, causing my heart to speed up.

"Still standing here," Joel said, interrupting us. "In fact, I'm feeling a little pervy just watching."

Tristan laughed. "Watch and learn, Grasshopper." He turned to me. "I called my mom and told her the theme to the dance is going to be Old Hollywood. She says if you want, you can borrow one of her vintage dresses. She has a gown that used to belong to Bette Davis back in the forties. My mom wore it to some awards show."

"Seriously?" I squeaked, bouncing up on my tiptoes. I hadn't even seen the dress, but I knew I wanted it. "I could kiss your mom."

"You can kiss me and I'll pass it along," Tristan promised. I planted a big smack on his lips.

"How did you know people would vote for Old Hollywood as the theme?" I asked.

"He also had his mom pick up Vivien Leigh's costume from *Gone with the Wind* in case everyone went with the Southern idea instead," Joel said. "It comes complete with a small black girl who follows you around to wave you with a fan."

Tristan gave Joel another shove, before smiling at me. "I knew you wanted Old Hollywood, which meant that's what I wanted."

"Ah, popularity. What you two want, the whole world wants. But what about me? I'm left still wanting ice cream," Joel said.

We headed out together. The guys offered to walk me back to my dorm in case any rogue security guards tried to get a photo of me, but I declined. I couldn't wait to tell my best friend, Kelsie, about the Bette Davis dress. She was going to freak out. She wants to be an actress and loves anything vintage Hollywood.

Joel was right, popularity has its advantages.

2

"I can*not* believe you get to wear a dress that was worn by Bette Davis. Do you have any idea how cool that is?" Kelsie flopped back onto her bed as if she were overcome by the enormity of it all.

"I know who she is, but I don't know if I ever saw any of her movies," I admitted. I was sitting on the floor with my laptop, trying to get our presentation to work.

"I can't believe you! Bette is like an icon. She was in *Dangerous* and *All About Eve*. Tons of stuff. She won two Oscars. The dress is totally wasted on you."

"Do you have any chocolate?" I asked as I typed.

"Nope."

I looked up in surprise. Kelsie always has chocolate in her room. Her dad is the CEO of a major candy corporation and has his assistant send her huge boxes full of stuff every month. "Your dad just sent some a few weeks ago. How can it all be gone?"

"I stuck it in the common room. I decided I didn't need the temptation." Kelsie sat up and smoothed her hands down her sides.

"You aren't going through a phase where you think you're fat, are you?"

"I don't think I'm fat. I know I'm fat." Kelsie squeezed a tiny quarter inch of flesh around her middle. "Even my face is fat."

"You're not fat. You look great. You just have a round face."

"Great, I have a circle for a head. Who doesn't love a girl who looks like a cartoon character?"

"I have a weird gap between my teeth," I pointed out with a smile, so she could see it. "Everyone has something about themselves they don't like. Your face is cute."

"I'm not going for cute. Besides, a tooth gap is sexy."

"You wouldn't think it was sexy if you knew how easy it is to get food wedged in there," I pointed out.

"See, it's even a food storage device, handy and sexy at the same time. This is why I'm doomed to be alone forever."

"Is this about the dance?" I closed the laptop, sensing a serious conversation was coming, one for which PowerPoint was not going to be needed. I had a feeling the birth of our nation wasn't what was on her mind. Our history project was going to have to wait.

"No one's asked me yet."

"You should ask Joel. Seriously, it would be like a favor. I think Mandy has designs on him."

"Joel is always my backup date. We go to everything together. I want a real date. I want romance, passion. You wouldn't understand; you've got Tristan."

"You say that like he's the best thing since sliced bread," I said with a laugh.

Kelsie turned so she was facing me. "You do realize how amazing he is, right? He's hot, he's crazy for you, his parents are famous. He *is* the best thing since sliced bread. I bet when sliced bread talks about something cool, it uses him as the example."

I paused. I knew Tristan was a great guy. I just wished everyone didn't think he was so wonderful all the time. People at school act like he's perfect. Sure he's good-looking, funny, sweet, his parents are famous, and he has money, but he always does this annoying thing where he cracks his knuckles. Not only does it sound gross, but it could also cause arthritis. And he's nice, but almost *too* nice sometimes. I couldn't discuss anything with him, because he would just agree with me and tell me to do whatever I wanted. When we went out to eat, he left it up to me, saying he didn't care if we went for sushi or pizza. At the movie theater I always chose what we saw. He didn't get riled up about politics, or movies, or sports. He was so calm about everything that he made Gandhi look like he'd had an anger management problem. It wasn't that I wanted him to lose it and start screaming, but it would have been nice if once in a while he had an opinion. If I wanted a heavy discussion, I had it with Joel, who could be counted on to have an opinion about everything. However, it's hard to explain that your boyfriend can be too agreeable. No one feels sorry for you.

"You're right. Tristan is definitely bread-worthy, and I have every confidence that you will find your own bread man who will love you exactly as you are," I assured Kelsie.

Kelsie smiled at me. "There are KitKats in my bottom desk drawer."

I gave a whoop and crawled forward so I could reach her desk. Buried under a stack of folders was a package of candy bars. I tossed one to her before opening my own. "I thought you said you gave your stash away," I said.

"I did. This is different. It's an emergency fund," Kelsie explained, biting into her candy bar.

"This counts as an emergency? You've got a pretty low threshold."

"I'm an Evesham girl. Anytime I want something, it counts as an emergency," Kelsie said with a smirk. "For someone who is so keen on emergency planning, I would think you would know this."

"Well, with the crisis averted, are you ready to get back to the presentation?"

Kelsie threw herself back down onto the bed. "I hate this project. Why are they trying to ruin our senior year? We're under a lot of stress, and stuff like this could drive us over the edge. They're crushing our college dreams. I think senior year should be pass/fail."

"You're not going to college," I pointed out. "You're doing an acting class through the art center next year. How stressed can you be?"

"That's not the point. I could be going to college, and maybe I would have, if the whole thing wasn't so stressful. Not everyone is like you, Miss Ivy League."

"I'm not in yet."

Kelsie waved away my stress about getting into Yale (top choice) and Harvard (close second) with a flip of her hand. "You'll get in. You're the kind of student that admissions counselors have wet dreams over. You're spending your summer curing lepers, for crying out loud."

"They're not lepers. I keep telling you it's a study for people with hepatitis. The pharmaceutical company my dad works for is doing a summer training program for doctors."

"Whatever. If you ask me, the question is, why do you want to go to college at all? It sounds like four more years of the same thing as here—boring classes, homework, and lots of brick buildings."

"My mom went to Yale, and I've always wanted to go there."

"If I were you, I would swing by the college bookstore, pick up a sweatshirt, and then join Tristan."

Tristan wasn't planning to go to college yet either. He said he was taking a gap year to think about what he wanted to do next, but I wasn't sure if he would ever go. He seemed perfectly content to drift. His plan for the summer and next year was to travel to the different homes his parents had around the world. It wasn't like Tristan was ever going to have to worry about getting a job, so he didn't need a degree, and learning for learning's sake wasn't really his thing.

"Summer with Tristan would be good, but you have to admit my end-of-summer party will be amazing." My dad had arranged for me to be able to invite all my friends to stay in a five-star resort as one last blowout for our group. Everyone would be heading in different directions in the fall, so knowing we would have one last chance to be together was huge.

"Are you kidding me? Your summer party is already the event of the year, and it's still months away. All I'm saying is, spending the summer with Tristan in Paris wouldn't be a bad thing. In August you could swing by your dad's leper colony, put in an appearance, and then have the party."

"You know I can't do that. Part of the reason my dad arranged the party was because I'm doing an unpaid internship. It's his way of paying me back."

"I know you're looking forward to this summer with your dad, and I'm sure working for free is very rewarding in its own special way. I also get that you don't get to spend a lot of time with him, but passing up Paris? With Tristan? Croissants, fancy cheese that stinks, French wine . . ."

"I haven't spent a whole summer with my dad in forever. There is no amount of stinky cheese and wine that would make me give it up."

"And no amount of Tristan?"

"Not even Tristan." I smiled and opened my laptop. "Now back to our project. I've got a great idea for our presentation that pulls together everything. We'll take the time line you did that shows the major battles and generals and combine it with the pictures I downloaded. It will totally support the position paper I drafted."

Kelsie's eyes slid away, and she suddenly became fascinated by a microscopic chip in the polish on her thumbnail.

"Kels?" My stomach started to sink, and I felt the KitKat boiling in a rush of acid.

"I need to talk to you about the time line."

"You didn't do it?" I had deliberately given Kelsie the job of doing the time line because it was the easiest part of the project. It was time consuming, but not hard. I'd done all the research and written the paper, not to mention the bulk of the presentation.

"I started it." Kelsie pulled out a notebook. She had a line drawn on the page. Down the side it read: *War starts, Washington crosses the Delaware in the snow, War ends, Create Declaration of Independence.* I closed my eyes.

"I know I'm missing a bunch of stuff, but I can finish it now while you work on the presentation," Kelsie said.

"The Declaration of Independence happened at the beginning of the revolution," I pointed out, proving so far that 25 percent of what she had down on the page was wrong.

"Really?" Kelsie looked down, surprised, at her history textbook. The binding didn't looked like it had been cracked yet. "Don't be pissed," she said.

"The project is fifty percent of our grade. Our presentation is *tomorrow*. Why didn't you tell me that you didn't think you would get your part done?" I wanted to kick myself. I loved Kelsie, but I knew what she was like. I should have made her show me her progress at least a week ago.

"Because I totally planned to finish it. Look, I'll talk to Ms. Brown and tell her the time line part was mine and not to have it reflect on your grade." Kelsie raised her right hand as if she were about to swear an oath.

I sighed. Kelsie knew I wouldn't let her take the fall. Besides, knowing Ms. Brown, all that would happen if Kelsie confessed is that we would get a lecture on the importance of teamwork and how learning to work together was part of the assignment. I felt like screaming, but yelling at Kelsie would be like kicking a puppy. I forced myself to take a deep breath.

"Okay. Make some coffee and do as much of the time line as you can while I work on the presentation. Then I'll take everything back to my room and polish it up." We both knew when I said "polish," what I really meant was that I would stay up until the wee hours getting it done.

Kelsie clapped her hands together and jumped off her bed. "Deal. I'll fire up the cappuccino machine in the lounge and make you a killer latte." She stopped in her doorway. "I'll make this up to you," she promised.

"Don't worry about it." I knew Kelsie. She wasn't the kind to clog up her brain with a lot of worry and stress anyway, so it was better to be nice about it. She believed stress led to break-outs, and she wasn't going to risk a zit for a war that happened hundreds of years ago. Freaking out was more my domain. I grabbed an extra KitKat. I was going to need the sugar rush to get through the night.

3

I wasn't always someone who worried about everything. As a kid I assumed things would generally work out okay. My mom took care of everything. She could banish the monsters under my bed, and if I fell off my bike, she would blow on my skinned knees, which magically made them hurt less. At that age I was unaware of the dangers of septicemia (blood poisoning) and was content with a Band-Aid. Now I buy Neosporin in bulk.

While my mom was great, I thought my dad was a hero. I used to be a total daddy's girl. When I was growing up, he would take me out on Saturday afternoons so my mom could have some time to herself. He would pick me up at my bedroom door with flowers. He would always plan something for us to do, but not little-kid stuff. He would take me to fancy restaurants, the planetarium, or to the art museum. We even went to the opera a couple of times. He asked me my opinion and really listened to what I had to say.

My dad used to say that he wanted to spend all the time he could with me, because once I became a teenager, I wouldn't want to hang out with him anymore. That's not how it worked out in the end. My mom died when I was twelve. She was supposed to pick me up from school, but she didn't show up. I wasn't worried. My mom was the übermom. She made her own bread, sewed princess costumes for me to play dress-up in, and was never, ever late. A teacher found me sitting on the steps of the school hours later and called my dad when she couldn't reach my mom. The teacher wanted to know why I'd waited so long without talking to anyone. I didn't know how to explain that it didn't occur to me that anything might be really wrong. That was the last time I can remember ever feeling completely safe.

A drunk driver hit my mom. She had bought fancy decorated cupcakes for my gymnastics club meeting and was running across the street to her car. He was rushing home after spending the afternoon in the bar. She was in the crosswalk and it was a bright sunny day. There was no reason for him to have hit her, no reason for her not to have dodged out of his way. The police officer told my dad it was just a case of bad luck. She was in the wrong place at the wrong time. There were a zillion variables that might have changed things. If she hadn't stopped at the bakery, if the baker hadn't been so busy and forced her to wait, if she had stopped before crossing the street instead of assuming anyone coming would stop, if he had taken a cab instead of driving drunk, or had gone an alternate way. I used to lie in bed at night and think of all the ways it could have gone differently. Unfortunately, real life isn't a choose-your-own-adventure book where you can go back and start over if you don't like how things turned out. I overheard my grandma telling our neighbor that the man hit my mom with such speed that it knocked her right out of her shoes. They figured she was dead before she hit the pavement. There was pink frosting and sprinkles in her hair.

My grandparents moved in for a few weeks right after Mom died, to take care of things and help arrange the funeral. The first couple of days, my dad didn't even come out of his room. I would walk slowly past his bedroom, and he would be lying there staring up as if he could see straight through the ceiling into the sky and all the way to heaven, where my mom would be looking back. There were whispered conversations where my grandfather would tell him to "pull yourself together." My dad eventually came out of his bedroom, but he wasn't the same. He went back to work, and my grandma hired a nanny, even though I kept insisting I was old enough to take care of myself after school.

The day my grandparents left, my grandma took me out for lunch so we could have some "girl time." She told me that my dad was going to be okay, but that he needed my help. It was important that I be very good and not cause him any extra difficulty. I took what she said to heart and set out to be the best kid in the entire country. I made my bed every morning and went to bed promptly at nine thirty without having to be told. I washed my dishes out in the sink and put them in the dishwasher as soon as I finished eating. I flossed every day; I could have been the poster child for the American Dental Association, my teeth were so clean. If my mom had come back to life, she wouldn't have recognized me.

It was around that time that I started collecting information and statistics on risk factors, and avoided anything that I deemed too dangerous. It was like what happened with my mom opened my eyes to just how easy it was for something bad to happen. I wanted to create a safety net out of rules and systems. If I did everything right, then I could keep anything horrible from ever happening again.

The spring after she died I was mastering how to cook. Ms. Lindsey, the nanny, was teaching me the basics. After school she and I would make something together, and then all I had to do was heat it up for dinner.

I remember very clearly when the next ball dropped. I was sure my dad would say something about that night's dinner choice. I'd made a homemade green chicken curry. Thai food had always been his favorite. I placed the dish down in front of him and managed to hold in my desire to say *Ta-da!*

"I've got some good news," he said, shoveling a bite into his mouth.

I plunked down in my chair and inhaled the smell of the

curry. I was hoping my dad was going to say something about summer vacation plans, since everyone I knew had exciting things lined up already.

"I've been checking around, and your grandma put in some calls to work her magic," he said, drawing out the suspense.

Maybe we would all rent a beach house on the Outer Banks together like we had years before. We could meet the boats when they came in and buy shrimp by the bucket. I could show my grandparents how I had learned to cook, and my dad could sit on the beach all day reading mystery novels. My dad would call me his Spanish peanut because my skin would turn a reddish brown from all the sun. I would sleep so well because of the sound of the waves outside that I wouldn't even notice all the sand in my bed or that my mom wasn't with us. I knew if we could only keep busy, then there wouldn't be time to let how different things were sink in. A new location meant Dad and I might not keep bumping into things that reminded us of her. I was so busy imagining the taste of salt water and burnt marshmallows that it took my brain a second to understand what my dad actually said.

"Boarding school?" I repeated, my fork falling onto the plate.

"Evesham Academy. It's one of the most elite schools in the country."

"I've never heard of it."

He laughed. "It's in Vermont."

"We're moving to Vermont?" My brain was still scrambling

to catch up. I'd left it down on the beach in North Carolina, and I couldn't make sense of anything.

"It's a boarding school. I think I'm a bit too old to fit in." He gave a forced chuckle. "It will be a great experience for you and set you up to go to any college in the country."

"I don't want to live in Vermont."

"You've never been to Vermont," my dad pointed out. Like a person has to go somewhere to know if they would like it or not. If he told me that we were moving to hell, would I have to stop by and take a tour before I decided if it was too hot for my taste? Parent logic doesn't always make sense.

"But I like living here."

My dad took my hand and held it. "The house is too much for me on my own."

I didn't point out that he wasn't on his own. We were together. "Is it the yard work? We could get a gardener." We already had a housekeeper who came every other day and did all the cleaning and grocery shopping. I didn't like the idea of my dad doing all the mowing anyway, especially since I was coming to realize how many mower accidents occurred in a year.

"It's not the yard, Hailey. It's . . ." His voice trailed off, and I knew he was thinking about my mom. My throat pulled tight, making it hard to swallow. "I'm going to put the house on the market and find something in the city closer to work."

"I wouldn't mind living in the city," I said quickly. "It would be really cool. We could get a place in one of those high-rise buildings that have a view of Lake Michigan. One with giant floor-to-ceiling windows."

"The schools in the city aren't good, and you wouldn't want to be cooped up in an apartment all the time while I'm at work. Evesham has a great reputation. This way, there will be tons of people your own age, lots of fresh air. They have all kinds of stuff to do, like archery and horseback riding."

Archery? Did he think I wanted to be Robin Hood? Sharp pointy sticks hurled at a high rate of speed, and no full body armor? I didn't think so. I opened my mouth to tell him no way, I wasn't going to go and he couldn't make me. I looked into his eyes. My dad was staring at me, and I could see the tension in his jaw despite his plastered-on smile. He kept swallowing. He looked like he was one step away from putting his head down on the table and crying. The kind of crying where you can't stop once you start.

"The school sounds great, Dad," I managed to choke out. I told myself maybe it would be just a year. Time for him to feel better. Then I would move home and we could go back to the way things were.

His face relaxed slightly, and I could see him take a deep breath. "Wait until you see the pictures of the place. It looks like a mini-Harvard, all those great stone buildings with lots of ivy. Some of the dorms even have fireplaces."

"Neat." I pushed my rice around on the plate. I wasn't remotely hungry anymore.

"And I checked out the science program in particular. State-of-the-art labs, and the teachers can help you organize an independent study on pretty much anything. They've also got some arrangement with the local college to use their materials if needed."

"Wow." My voice sounded flat to me, but my dad didn't seem to notice. He'd gone back to eating his dinner with gusto. "I'd come home in the summer, though, right?" I asked. "We'll spend our summers and vacations together?"

My dad smiled. "Of course we will." He took another big bite of the curry. "Wherever you ordered this from is amazing. Best curry I've had in years. Be sure to stick their menu on the fridge."

I started to tell him I'd made the curry myself, but then it didn't seem to matter. It didn't matter any more than his promise that we'd spend holidays together.

4

Despite what my dad had promised about spending summers together, there was always a reason it made more sense for me to go to my grandparents' house—some project he had to work on, or construction in his new condo building.

This year was going to be different. When he asked me what I wanted as a graduation gift, I told him I wanted to have the whole summer together before I went to college. He seemed surprised, but he agreed. He even arranged the job for me with his company so I'd have something on my résumé besides working at the Gap. It was also his idea to throw the end-of-summer party. It was going to be the perfect summer. We'd have lots of stuff to talk about from working together, and after a few weeks it would start to seem easier. When I was a kid, I never ran out of things to say to him, and I was sure if we could just spend more than a day or two together, it would go back to that easy comfort. I could picture us sitting on the balcony of the resort, our feet up on the railing, talking about college and what I might end up doing, maybe even talking about my mom. I could picture him sitting at the pool with all of my friends, getting to know them. I'd been dating Tristan for almost four years, and my dad had only met him twice. Most of the time he called him Taylor by accident.

I unlocked the door to my dorm room and plopped everything down onto my bed. My room was in Elsie Hall, built in the 1920s. There was wood paneling on one wall, and the floors were a gray slate. It had one of the fireplaces my dad had seen in the brochure, although there was a strict no-fire rule. I'd put a collection of candles in the hearth. We were allowed to paint our rooms, and I'd painted the other three walls a thick cream color that reminded me of French vanilla ice cream.

Kelsie had gotten practically nothing done on the time line, and what she did have completed, I wasn't sure I could trust. Knowing Kelsie, she would have General Electric listed as one of the leaders, along with Captain Kangaroo. She was a great friend and would lend you her last cashmere sweater, but academics weren't her thing. I was mad at her for not coming through, and even more mad that I felt I couldn't tell her I was upset, because of how she would react. She would make it into a huge drama and fall over herself to apologize. It would take me longer to sort it out than it would to do the project myself. If we stood any chance of acing American History, it was going to be up to me. It was going to be an all-nighter if I was going to get it done. I pulled off my shirt and yanked on my mom's old Yale sweatshirt. I thought that I might as well be comfortable.

I wandered down to our common room to get a bottle of water. I couldn't do anything about missing sleep, but at least I could stay hydrated. Dehydration can lead to kidney failure. Also, it's bad for your skin. Besides, if I had any more coffee, I was going to get the shakes. There was a group of freshmen piled all over the lounge. They had a movie on the TV and were doing facials and painting one another's nails. Their giggling stopped when I walked into the room.

"Hey, Hailey, you want to watch a movie with us?"

I looked over. It was some slasher flick. I never saw the point in horror movies. Real life is bad enough without having someone chopping you up in your dreams as a form of entertainment. "Sorry, guys. I've got homework."

"Is it true you went to the Oscars last year with Tristan's parents?" a bucktoothed girl asked me, her mouth hanging open.

"No. They limit how many people can get into those award shows. Tristan and I just went with them to some of the after parties."

"Oh my god, that is still so cool. Did you meet anyone famous?" The group of freshman girls was now in a circle around me. I felt like someone who had introduced fire to a group of cavemen.

I pulled a bottle of water out of the fridge and wiped it clean with a paper towel. You don't even want to know what kind of germs are on those things. You might as well clamp your mouth down on a toilet. "Sure. We ate dinner with Johnny Depp. It was cool, but once you meet a few of them, you realize famous people aren't really any different from anyone else." This was true. Tristan's parents once invited me to a dinner party they had, and the guy next to me had been in a zillion box office hits, but apparently didn't know basic oral hygiene, because his breath smelled like a sewer grate. "Have fun with your movie." I raised my water bottle as a good-bye gesture.

"You can't go. Stay and tell us more about who you've met, and I'll do your nails," one girl said.

"No can do. History project due tomorrow." I turned to leave, but the girl grabbed my arm to try to convince me. She must have forgotten that she was still holding a bottle of nail polish, because a spray of bright red polish glopped onto my sleeve. We both looked down at the paint.

"Oh my god. I am so sorry." She wiped at the polish, smearing it over a larger area.

I yanked my arm back. This was my mom's sweatshirt. The one she wore when she went to Yale. It was one of the only things of hers that I had with me at school. Tears rushed into my eyes. It was ruined.

"I'm such a spaz. I'll buy you a new shirt." The freshman girl looked like she was ready to start crying too. The other girls had taken a slight step away from her in order to distance themselves from her certain social suicide. I swallowed the tight knot in my throat. She hadn't meant to do anything. It was my own fault. I shouldn't have worn the shirt if I didn't want anything to ever happen to it.

"It's okay," I managed to whisper. I waved her hands away before she could smear the polish further. "I really have to get going." I hustled back down the hall to my room.

I shut my door behind me and slid down to the floor. I couldn't believe that had happened. I pulled off the sweatshirt and looked at the stain. I buried my face into the shirt. I bet my mom would have known how to get nail polish out in the wash. Today was turning into a crappy day. I would have gladly traded the Bette Davis dress to have my mom's faded sweatshirt back without a big blob of Candy Apple Red Kiss on it.

I looked over at the clock. It was getting late. I knew I could either lie on the floor and feel sorry for myself or I could get working on the stupid time line so I could get at least a few hours of sleep. I fired up my computer, and there was the *ping* indicating new mail. It was from my dad. I clicked on it with a smile; his e-mails always put me in a good mood. But as soon as I read the first few lines, my stomach clenched tight.

Hailey—

I hope your classes are going well. I have some bad news; there's been a change of plans. I've been asked to teach a lecture series in London. The company is going to sponsor the program, and it's an excellent public relations move. It will likely result in an increase in funding for several projects. This means someone else will be heading up the training project in Tahoe this summer.

I hate to cancel our plans, but I know you'll understand. I've talked to your grandparents, and they would love to have you again. I called in a favor and was able to get you a job in the Munson Hospital Lab up there. Heck, you'll get to spend your whole summer at the beach. You won't even notice I'm not there. My lectures will wrap up in August, and we can spend some time together then, and we'll pick you out whatever you like for a graduation present. About the party you planned, your grandparents can't have all your friends at the house, but you could invite a few of them. I bet they'll love the beach too! Besides, sometimes a small group can be more fun than having everyone.

Love,
Dad

I stared at the computer screen. I hoped that if I stared long enough, the words would rearrange themselves into a different message. This couldn't be happening. He was canceling. I'd done everything I could do to be the perfect daughter, and it still didn't matter. I felt like I was going to throw up, that sour slick of spit sticking in the back of my throat. I picked my iPod up off the bed and hurled it across the room. It left a scar on the wood and made a clunk when it hit the floor. That made me feel a little bit better. I looked around for something else to destroy. I grabbed my pillow and yanked open the drawer in my desk, pulling it almost completely out. I took the scissors and stabbed them into the center of the pillow. That's what I thought of his fancy lecture series and his acting like changing my party plans was no big deal. I stabbed the pillow again. A poof of tiny white down feathers flew out, and as I pulled out the scissors, more began floating up into the air. I felt my breath coming faster.

I stood up and kicked my mom's sweatshirt out of my way so I didn't have to look at the ruined sleeve. I took my bag and turned it upside down, dumping everything onto the floor. I shoved my history book out of my way, snatched my cell phone from the pile, and immediately called Tristan. His cell didn't pick up. He never charged the damn thing. What was the point of having a cell phone if you didn't have it on when people needed to reach you? I was so frustrated, I wanted to scream. I scrolled through my list and stabbed a button. Joel picked up on the first ring.

"Is Tristan there?"

"Hi, this is Joel. Nice talking to you. Usually when people call my phone, they're calling to talk to me."

"I need to talk to Tristan." My voice snagged on the words. Suddenly the anger was sharing space with tears. I was even madder that I felt like crying.

"Hey, are you okay?" Joel's voice turned soft. "Tristan's not here."

"Where is he?" My voice came out small. "Can you get him? I really need him."

"He's in a study group down in our lounge. He's not supposed to be back until late. Do you want me to get him?"

The tears started to pour out of my eyes, laser hot as they slid down my face.

"Hailey? You still there? What's wrong?"

"I . . ." My voice trailed off. I didn't know how to explain it. How it hurt that my dad didn't want me around, and how it was even more upsetting that I'd let myself be so excited about the summer, when I should have known better. "You tell him I called?" I squeaked out.

"Yeah. I'll tell him to call you the second he walks in. Listen, you can talk to me about whatever . . ."

I clicked off the phone without even saying good-bye. My feet tapped on the floor. I couldn't just sit there. I felt like I was going to fly apart into a thousand pieces. I yanked my door open and stepped out into the hallway right into the path of our dorm matron, Ms. Estes.

"Ms. Kendrick," she said in her clipped voice.

"I have to go out for a bit."

"I'm afraid it's after eleven." She pointed to her naked wrist as if she were wearing a watch. Evesham required all students to be in their dorms from eleven p.m. to six a.m. on weeknights. No exceptions.

"I—I need to get some air." I could feel myself shaking. She stood there, unmoving. Ms. Estes had never met a rule she didn't like to enforce. I wanted to push her out of my way, but instead I stepped back into my room and slammed my door closed.

"Two demerit points, Ms. Kendrick." I heard her say through the door. Without even seeing her, I knew she was writing it down in the small Snoopy notebook she carried in her pocket, just for these occasions. I kicked the door when I was sure she was far enough down the hall not to hear. My toe gave a loud crack. I bit down to avoid yelling out. I hopped around on one foot. It felt like I had broken my big toe.

I hobbled back and forth in front of my bed, trying to shake off the pain. My phone rang, and I lunged over to grab it. *Thank God, Tristan.* I looked at the display. It wasn't Tristan; it was Joel. I threw it back down onto the bed without picking up the call. It felt like I couldn't get a deep breath. I yanked open the window and took deep greedy gulps of air. I don't remember making the decision. There wasn't a go-or-don't-go pause. It's hard to know what would have happened if I had stopped to think, but I didn't. One second I was in the room, and the next I was climbing down the ivy outside the window, jumping the last few feet down to the ground. I stood outside for a beat, looking back at the warm yellow light of my room, and then I took off.

5

The problem with running away at Evesham was that there really wasn't anywhere to go. It wasn't because the campus has a giant wall around it, though it does, but because the school is several miles outside of town. Wandering around in the woods on a dark and drizzling night didn't feel like getting away with anything. It just felt wet and cold.

I paused by the front gate, next to a giant statue of the school mascot, a knight in armor holding a sword pointing toward the sky. Everyone on campus called him the Tin Man. Evesham was named after a famous battle in England in the thirteenth century. The Evesham motto—"Loyalty, Duty, and Honor"—was inscribed in brass letters around the statue's base.

That was a laugh. Loyalty and duty. Look how far that had gotten me. I was always was the one who smoothed things over, who gave in to make things work. The school could act like loyalty and duty were virtues, but my experience had taught me that all it made you was a doormat. I bent over and picked up a clot of wet mud. I stared at the statue, almost expecting the knight to beg me to reconsider, but he just stood there with his smug unreadable expression. I pulled back and let the mud fly. It smacked him in the head with a surprisingly loud *splat*.

"Screw loyalty," I said, hurling another ball of mud. "And duty, too." I was bending over, scooping handfuls of mud, and throwing them as fast as I could at the statue. I was a lousy athlete most of the time, but rage was doing a great job of improving my aim. The mud was sliding down the side of the statue, and occasionally a *ping* would ring out as a rock hit the metal.

"Whoa. What did he do to you?" a voice said behind me.

I whirled around, ready to bolt. I could make out a figure in the dark but couldn't see his face clearly. He took a step forward. It was Joel.

I dropped the clot of mud in my hand. My jeans were coated in grime, and I could tell it was in my hair, too. I looked over my shoulder at the statue in case he had anything to add that might help me explain.

"I came to make sure you were okay," Joel said, his voice calm and slow as if he were speaking to someone who might snap at any moment, which, given the circumstances, was probably a good strategy. "I tried calling you back a few times, but you didn't pick up."

"I'm not okay," I said, my voice small.

He didn't say anything else. Joel crossed the few feet that separated us and pulled me into a hug, despite the fact that I was soaking wet and dirty. "It's all right. You're going to be okay, though, I promise."

I leaned into the hug, and he squeezed me tight before pulling away and plunking me down on the closest bench. I started bawling like a two-year-old and then spilled the whole story about my relationship with my dad and everything else that had happened. "I know it's no big deal. In the big scheme of things, we're talking summer plans, not starving children or a collapsing world economy or anything." I shrugged, hoping to give the impression that I was working myself closer to sanity and off the emotional edge.

"It seems like a big deal to me. He gave you his word. He made a promise."

"But this conference is a big deal. He'll have a chance to pull in all sorts of funding."

"But he had you make all these plans and invite all these people over for a summer blowout, only to leave you in a lurch. Besides, this is still his last chance to have time with you before you go off to college."

"Yeah, but I'm not going to school in Borneo or anything. I could still come home during the summers." I wiped my nose with my sleeve.

"Are you trying to convince me or yourself?" Joel asked. I jumped a bit at the unexpected question. He laughed at my expression. "You're busted, Kendrick. You're ticked. It's fine to be pissed at your dad. Anger isn't a bad thing."

"I'm not mad. I'm disappointed," I clarified.

Joel laughed harder. "Disappointed, huh? Do you always hurl things at statues when you're disappointed?"

I looked at my hands. They were covered in mud, and I had broken two fingernails. Busted. I was mad. In fact, it was possible I had left mad behind, whipped through angry, and was plunk in the middle of really pissed off. I had been *disappointed* that my dad seemed fine with me living far away at boarding school. I felt *let down* that when I got straight A's, won state championships in debate, and made student government, all he did was pat me absently on the head like a good puppy who had managed to bring back a stick without peeing on the rug. I was *bummed* that my dad was so disinterested in my life that he could barely remember the names of my friends when he did see me, but this was a whole new level of ticked off. I felt my eyes fill up with tears again.

"He's my dad, and he acts like he wants to forget I even exist."

"No one could forget you." Joel tipped my chin up so we were looking eye to eye. "You're the kind of person that makes an impression."

"What kind of impression? Sometimes I feel like I'm not even being me. That everything is this big show. The amazing Hailey Kendrick. The worst part is, I'm trying to impress someone who isn't even paying attention, and I don't even know who I really am. I wander around here like I'm starring in a reality show, always being nice and making sure my hair is perfect. I'm the Polly Perfect Popular girl."

"I can understand that." He caught my raised eyebrow. "You think that this is all there is to me? Good guy Joel? He's such a great sport, smart. Heck, he even dresses well. You can hardly tell he's the scholarship kid."

My face flushed red. Evesham is ridiculously expensive, and the school board funds a few scholarships for kids who come from underprivileged families. Most of the scholarship kids end up dropping out; they don't fit in. It isn't that people try to be snobby, at least most people. It's just hard to know what to talk about with them. You can't really bring up your holiday plans to the south of France when you know that their parents might be on welfare. It doesn't seem right. All the Evesham students might wear the same uniforms, but the scholarship kids never have designer handbags and shoes that were custom made in Italy. The kids who don't drop out tend to be loners. They don't even seem to want to hang out with each other. It's as if they don't want to create too large a target.

It was easy to forget Joel was there on scholarship. He wasn't anything like the others. He was always in the middle of everything, laughing and cracking jokes. He never seemed bitter, or like he resented what everyone else had.

"I never think of you as the scholarship kid," I said.

"My problem is that I can't get you to think of me at all," Joel said with an exaggerated wink, and he dodged when I tried to shove him in the side with my elbow. "Look, I know I'm lucky to be here at all. If you saw the public school where I grew up, you would think you were in Beirut. They have metal detectors at the door, the ceiling is always leaking—probably asbestos—and most of the teachers are only there because they couldn't get a job at any decent school. Going here is a huge opportunity, and I get that. It's going to mean getting into a good college and doing something with my life. People can say all they want that this is the land of opportunity, but the truth is, if you don't get a decent education, you're screwed."

"Is this going to be one of your policy points when you're president?"

"Better believe it. I'm going to make so many changes that they're going to have to find space on Mount Rushmore to carve my face in next to Lincoln and Washington."

"Guess your ego isn't on scholarship, huh?"

"I figure if I act like I'm so great, the rest of you will just assume it's the truth."

"It seems to be working pretty well so far."

"Yeah, but people around here are pretty easy to fool. Sheep, most of them. Present company excluded, of course."

"Of course."

"I don't mind appreciating how lucky I am to be here," he said, "but I do hate having to be so damn grateful all the time.

It's like anything I do has to come with a caveat, that I never would have been able to do it without the kind contributions of the alumni foundation. I can't even own my own success, you know? It's like I have to share it with everyone."

I thought about the alumni banquet Evesham holds every year at homecoming. There's always a big call for donations, and last year, Joel was one of the people who had to get up and talk about how much he'd benefited from his Evesham experience. It had never occurred to me how that might have made him feel.

I touched his shoulder. "I think you're pretty amazing, with or without the scholarship," I said. "In fact, I'm counting on you being elected president someday so I can get invited to all those swanky White House parties."

"Actually, I was thinking of making you my vice president. Lots of perks. You get your own office in the White House and everything. A jet, too. Not Air Force One, but still better than flying coach."

"The vice presidency isn't really my thing. I don't mind it on student council, but I can't see me doing it long term. I might take an ambassadorship, though. Someplace good, like France or England. I don't want to be stuck in some third world country and end up with malaria."

"I would feel terrible if you caught some intestinal parasite on our nation's behalf. I think we should plan to go with London, since you don't speak French."

"Thanks. Not just for the future ambassadorship, but for

sneaking out to find me. I feel better," I said, tucking a clump of my muddy hair behind one ear. I was still mad at my dad, but I didn't feel like I was going to fly into a thousand pieces anymore.

"This is all it takes to make you feel better?" Joel shook his head sadly, as if he couldn't believe me. "I think you should raise the bar."

"I don't know. Don't forget, I've pretty well beat up our buddy here." I pointed to the statue of the knight. "I would say I've struck a blow against duty and feeling fake."

Joel's smile turned up on one side, just the tiniest bit evil. "What do you say we strike a real blow?"

"See if you can wrap my sweatshirt around his head. Then push from up there while I pull," Joel called up to me. He was coated in mud now too. "Try to get as much leverage as you can."

We were trying to remove the mascot's head, but it was clear that this was one knight who didn't intend to be decapitated. I didn't have any artistic talent, so until that moment I'd had no appreciation for how much effort must go into making a statue. However they'd attached the head, it had clearly been done with more than a mere dollop of Elmer's glue. Whoever made these things made them to last. Our plan was to take his head off and mount it on the front gate of Evesham, but I was getting close to giving up.

I was straddling the knight's upraised arm a good six feet off the ground. I scootched forward so that I could take the sweatshirt from Joel without falling off. I wrapped it around the back of the knight's head. Joel grabbed a hold of the arms of the shirt and pulled down while I tried to push. It didn't feel as if the head was even budging. I didn't think this plan would work. Given that our earlier attempt, whacking his head with a large stick, hadn't seemed to do the trick, I didn't think we had the brute strength to just rip it off. The only impact we seemed to have made all night was a slight dent in his chin, but that might have been there before we'd started.

I leaned back against the upraised part of the knight's arm and tried to kick at his head. There was a loud *crack*, and the arm I was sitting on snapped off. It felt like I hung in the air for a split second, like the coyote in the Road Runner cartoons when he would run off a cliff. I let out a squeak, and then I fell.

Before I could hit the ground, Joel was under me, catching me with a loud "Oomph." He staggered under my sudden weight, but hung on, holding me as if he were the groom and we were headed over the threshold. We both looked up at the statue. He still had his head, but his arm had sheared right off. It was lying on the ground, the tip of the sword snapped clean off. Our eyes met, and we both started laughing.

I slipped down so that I was standing, but Joel still had his arms around me, holding me up. I was laughing so hard that my eyes were watering.

"I can't believe we did that," I said, slightly out of breath.

"I can't believe I'm going to do this."

I was about to ask what he meant, when he kissed me. He pulled me even closer, and I could feel the heat of him through our wet clothes. It was like he was on fire. His hands were on either side of my face. I wasn't aware of the knight, the rain, or the mud anymore. Joel was consuming every sense I had. His heat, the smell of his skin, the taste of his mouth, and the look in his eyes. It was as if the entire universe had shrunk down to the space that contained us. We were a black hole pulling everything in. I wound my hands in his hair and pulled him even closer, our bodies locking together like perfectly fitting puzzle pieces, LEGO bricks clicking together to build something bigger and better. I felt the rain hit my skin and then sizzle off.

"Hey!" A voice yelled out. My brain snapped into place. I was kissing Joel. What was I thinking? I yanked back, breaking contact with his lips. I started to spin around, and a flashlight clicked on, blinding me. I threw my arm up in front of my face to shield my eyes.

"What the heck are you kids doing?"

I felt so guilty that it took me a second to realize that the voice in the darkness was talking about the statue and not the fact that I was kissing my boyfriend's best friend. I tried to see who was past the light. It had to be one of the Evesham security guards. I wasn't sure how I was going to explain what had happened. No one would believe that the arm had just fallen off while we happened to be there making out.

Joel grabbed me by the wrist. "Run." He took off, lightning

fast, dragging me behind. It took me a few steps to get my feet moving in the right direction. Every time I nearly fell, Joel heaved me up by my arm and kept me running. It felt like my arm was going to tear out of the socket. He wove through the trees, staying away from any of the trails, to make it harder for the guard to follow. I could hear the branches snapping as we crashed through the woods. Behind us the guard stuck close at first, the beam of his flashlight bouncing as he ran. We were running faster, though, and I thought that Joel should have gone out for track. It was all I could do to keep up with him. After a few minutes the guard fell behind. Joel kept running long after I would have stopped. A thin branch smacked my face, stinging my cheek. I sucked in my breath. That hurt. My free hand reached up, and I felt blood.

Joel stopped quickly, and I ran into his back. We were both breathing fast. I bent over so I could suck a few deep breathes into my lungs. I rubbed my wrist where Joel had been holding me.

"I think we lost him," Joel panted.

"I can't believe we ran away."

"I don't think he'll be able to identify us. It's dark, and with all the mud, how much could he see? I don't think he could have gotten a really good look."

"We should get back, before anyone does a room check." I couldn't look directly into his eyes. Before he could reply, I started walking back toward the main part of campus. Joel walked behind me. He was so quiet that I had to fight the urge to turn around and make sure he was really there. That it, he, wasn't a dream. The whole situation seemed surreal—the statue, the kiss, getting caught. It was as if I had crawled through a portal and ended up in an alternate universe. I wouldn't have been surprised if a unicorn had wandered past to give us a ride.

When we got back to the dorms, we stood under my window. "If I boost you up onto my shoulders, do you think you can pull yourself in?" Joel asked, looking up to survey the height. "Otherwise we could try tapping on one of the lower windows and seeing if someone will let you in," he suggested. Both of us knew that option meant involving someone else in what had happened. I quickly decided that the last thing we needed was a witness.

"I think I can do it. Don't drop me, though, okay?"

"Look, about what happened . . . ," Joel began.

"It's no big deal. If the security guard identifies us, I'll talk to my dad. He can buy a new knight for this place."

"I didn't mean the statue." Joel looked serious; his face was set into hard lines. He wiped a smear of mud off my cheek and saw the cut. His eyebrows drew together in concern. "You're hurt."

"It's nothing. Just a scratch. Don't worry about it—or, you know, what happened. It didn't mean anything. Must have been all the endorphins from tearing the arm off that guy. Thrill of the hunt. You hear about that kind of thing happening all the time in battle." I looked away quickly, and hoped he couldn't tell that I was blushing.

"Yeah." Joel's voice was flat. "It was just an accident. I would never do anything to hurt Tristan. He's my best friend."

"I know. I don't want to hurt him either. Don't worry. I won't say anything. We can pretend the whole thing never happened."

"Is it really that easy? Just forget it and erase everything?"

"Exactly. Poof. Look at that—I've already forgotten." I waved my hands between us as if I were creating a magic spell. My heart was beating fast. Joel had to agree. If we told Tristan, he would be crushed. He would never understand. Heck, I didn't understand. I'd never had romantic feelings for Joel in all the years I'd known him. But that kiss . . . It was like I had been possessed.

Joel looked into the woods and said nothing. He rubbed his hand over his face and then took a step closer. My heart stopped dead in my chest. Was he going to try to kiss me again? He bent over, cupping his hands. "Step up. Let's get you back inside."

I let myself take a breath. It was forgotten. It was going to be okay. I stepped into his hands, and from there up onto his shoulders. I could feel the strength of his hands as they cupped my ankles, holding me steady. My hands scrambled to find something to hold on to. I was still a few inches short of the windowsill. The rocks in the walls didn't stick out far enough to make any sort of handhold, and I was afraid the ivy wouldn't hold me.

"I can't reach," I whispered down to him.

"Okay, hang on. Step onto my hands and I'll boost you up

farther." He gave a grunt and then raised his arms up above his head. I hugged the wall and stepped up. His arms were shaking with the effort, and I had the image of what it would be like if I fell and broke something. Luckily, the extra lift was enough and I was able to get a hold of the wooden sill for my room. I pulled myself up. Clearly I needed to do more chin-ups in gym, because my arms were screaming from the effort. My feet scraped on the stone wall searching for a bit of extra purchase. I didn't as much crawl into my room as fall in. Once I was inside, I leaned back out the window.

"You okay?" Joel asked.

"Uh-huh. You okay?" I couldn't see his face in the dim light, but I could make out his shape. He nodded. "Thanks for coming to find me."

"You can always count on me."

I wasn't sure what to say, so I waved to him and shut the window. I slid down the wall until I was sitting on the floor. It didn't feel like I could count on anything anymore.

7

One of things I don't like about Evesham is the shared bathrooms. There are two per floor in the dorms. It's not like they're nasty. You couldn't charge what Evesham costs and get away with chipped tile and laminate counters. The floors are heated, and there's a wide granite countertop vanity where everyone sits to do their makeup in the morning. It was designed to look like the washrooms they have in Harrods department store in London. My Evesham bathroom was nicer than the bathroom I had at home, and I wasn't even expected to clean it. Evesham has a fleet of janitors who swoop in and mop and polish it as soon as we're done in the mornings. There's never so much as a stray hair in the corner. The problem with the bathrooms at Evesham is that you can never be alone.

I closed my eyes and wished for total silence. It was impossible to block out the sounds of the girls who were singing in the shower and the two girls next to me who were breaking down the calorie count of every food item ever known to man. Another girl was standing behind me spraying clouds of some perfume that stuck to the back of my throat like an oily smear of crushed roses. I opened my eyes to glare at her in the mirror.

"I'm sorry, Hailey." She waved her hands around to try to get rid of the smell, but all that did was wave it into my face. "I should do this in my room. I don't know what I was thinking." She scurried out of the bathroom.

I leaned forward to look at myself closely. My foundation had almost completely hidden the scratch on my cheek. All anyone would be able to see was a faint pink line, and they wouldn't even see that unless they were looking really hard. I searched my face. I couldn't put my finger on it, but it seemed as if there had to be something else, something I wasn't seeing, that marked the events from last night. Maybe a giant I KISSED JOEL carved into my forehead. My mind kept replaying the kiss over and over like some demented TiVo.

"You okay?"

I jumped and spun around. "What are you doing here?" I asked. Kelsie's room was on the other end of the floor, and she usually used the other bathroom.

Kelsie stopped short. "Whoa. Someone woke up cranky. I came to bring you a Starbucks. I bribed one of the juniors to make a run. It's my way of saying sorry again for the history project thing." She held out a cup for me.

My mind went blank for a second. I had completely forgotten about our history project. It was like something that had happened in another lifetime. When I'd gotten back to my room the night before, I'd felt like I had run a string of marathons. I had pulled my muddy clothes off, dumped them into the hamper, and crawled into bed without even taking the time to brush my teeth.

I hadn't done a thing on our project. The time line wasn't done. The presentation wasn't even close to done. We were screwed. I opened my mouth to tell her what had happened last night, and then clicked it shut. It wasn't that I didn't trust her. I told Kelsie everything. We'd been best friends since freshman year. It wasn't like she expected me to be perfect, but I couldn't escape the feeling that she wouldn't approve of what had happened. Not that she *should* approve. Even I knew that kissing Joel back was a lousy thing to do. I had lain in bed earlier that morning thinking about it after my alarm had gone off. I liked Joel, I really did. But not like that. He was always teasing how he was crazy for me, but it was just a running joke. He never meant anything by it. If he did, he surely wouldn't have joked about it right in front of Tristan. Besides, even if we did like each other, it wasn't like it would work out. He was best friends with Tristan. The kiss was just a onetime thing. There had been all that emotion, and then Joel had talked about how he felt like an outsider, and things had just happened. Besides, Joel and I had already decided that we were going to blot out the event altogether. If I told Kelsie, even if I told her only part of the story, it would make it real again.

Plus, there was the fact that Kelsie couldn't keep her mouth shut. She was an awesome friend, but she wasn't the kind of person who had a big future ahead of her in keeping secrets. It was safe to say the CIA wouldn't be recruiting her anytime soon. She was just incapable of keeping a good story to herself.

"Earth to Hailey," Kelsie said, interrupting my thoughts.

I blinked a few times and saw Kelsie staring at me with concern in her eyes. "Sorry. My dad and I had a fight last night and it's playing with my head."

Kelsie yanked out the plush stool next to mine and plunked down. "You and your dad never fight. What happened? Was he screaming? My dad yells so hard that the vein in his forehead looks like it's going to pop out of his head. I think it's all the sugar he eats at his job. It makes him really high strung."

"Well, I guess it wasn't really a fight. There was no yelling or anything. In fact, we didn't even talk."

"So this was, like, an imaginary fight?" One of Kelsie's eyebrows went up.

"He sent me an e-mail. He's canceling our summer plans. He's going to England for some conference."

"What about the party? Everybody's already planning on going."

I felt a rush of anger. The party? That was the first thing

she thought of, how it would affect her and her summer plans? "There isn't going to be any party," I spat out.

Kelsie touched my arm softly. "I'm sorry. I know how much you were looking forward to the whole curing lepers thing. On the upside, now you can go traveling with Tristan all summer. Think about how amazing that will be. Be a glass-full kind of person."

"Yeah."

"Wow. Try to keep down the enthusiasm there. Oh, the horrors you have to deal with, a whole summer in Europe with the cutest guy in the world, who's insane for you. How will you manage? The UN should totally step in and do something. Maybe some celebrities could band together and hold a telethon. If you ask me, the big problem you have is telling everyone the party's canceled. People are going to be seriously bummed. I know a few people booked flights and vacations around the plan. I wonder if Tristan can talk to his folks and see if they'll host it. I bet if you asked him, he'd clear it with them."

"I didn't get our project done," I said, changing the subject.

Kelsie's face wrinkled up. "What do you mean you didn't get it done?"

"I had the fight with my dad and I forgot. We'll have to ask Ms. Brown for an extension."

"She automatically drops two grades for an extension. That means at best we get a C."

"What? Is it going to ruin your chances to get into your acting class?" I yanked my brush through my hair. *Now* she was all worried about our history grade? Where was the concern when she was supposed to be getting the time line done?

Kelsie held up both of her hands. "Don't snap my head off. I brought up the grade because of how you get about it. A C is fine with me. Heck, it's a step up from what I'm getting in French."

I felt suddenly deflated, like someone had sucked all the energy out of my body. "I'm sorry. The thing with my dad got to me."

Kelsie put her hand back on my shoulder. I could see both of us in the mirror. "I bet if you told Ms. Brown what happened, she wouldn't mark you down. You're her favorite by a mile. You're the only one who does the suggested additional reading in that class. It's clear you actually like history. You're the daughter she always wanted to have. Besides, if she doesn't change your grade, you can blame your dad and maybe he'll feel guilty enough to buy you a car for graduation."

I looked at my watch. "We better hurry or we'll be late for assembly."

Kelsie threw her arm around me as we walked down the hall. "Don't stress, Hail. What is it you're always saying? Things happen for a reason."

Evesham starts every day with an all-school assembly. The official reason is tradition. The administration liked to "bring us together as a community" and start the day with a "shared vision." Near as I could tell, the real reason we do it is because our dean, Mr. Winston, likes to be the center of attention. The school is nondenominational, but I'm pretty sure Mr. Winston secretly wants to be one of those evangelical ministers. Every day he starts with an inspirational story or quote, before diving into the various announcements about clubs and the importance of people being careful not to toss their silverware into the trash when they dump their trays in the lunchroom.

Most people would have preferred to have an extra fifteen minutes of sleep, but I usually didn't mind assembly. There's something relaxing about the sameness of it. The pews we sit in always smell like lemon polish, and the large arched windows make the hall feel important, like a cathedral. That morning I almost wished it were a church. I would need to do some serious praying if I were going to be able to get Ms. Brown to give us an extension with no penalty. History was my favorite subject. I felt like it should be science, since that was my dad's thing, but deep down it mattered more to me how I did in history.

Kelsie and I were two of the last people to walk into the assembly hall. We slipped into the back row just as Mr. Winston was taking his place at the lectern. My eyes skimmed over the crowd. Girls and guys sat on opposite sides of the hall, seniors in the back, with the younger grades closest to the front so the teachers could keep a close eye on them. Tristan caught my eye. His hair was still wet from the shower. He winked at me, and I found myself smiling. Then I noticed Joel was right next to him, and my heart skipped a beat. Joel looked at me and then pointed at his watch, shaking his head. Kelsie flipped him off, and I felt the tight band around my chest loosen. It was going to be okay.

Kelsie pulled her iPhone out of her bag and held it in her lap, where none of the teachers would see it. She liked to check celebrity blogs during assembly.

"I'm afraid there is a serious issue we need to discuss this morning," Mr. Winston said.

"Holy shit," someone whispered a few rows in front of me. I looked up and saw Mr. Winston standing with Mr. Hanson, the football coach, who was holding the metal arm from the knight.

A few people started to giggle, but stopped as Mr. Winston's gaze fell on them.

"That is priceless," Kelsie whispered to me.

"People, this is not a joke. I see no reason for laughter. This statue is a symbol of this institution. It stands for the values that this school is based upon. It was a gift from a benefactor from the 1950s. This crime is a slap in the face of every student here."

"How the hell did they get the arm off? They must have had a blowtorch," Kelsie said, leaning forward to see the arm better.

I shrugged. I wondered if I'd left any fingerprints on the statue. Would the school have some sort of CSI crew that could dust it? Crime wasn't my usual thing. I had never even stolen a Tootsie Roll from the bulk section of the grocery store. I could feel myself starting to sweat.

"I would like the guilty parties to do the honorable thing and stand up and admit to their crime," Mr. Winston said. People looked around to see if anyone felt honorable. My butt felt glued to the seat. My eyes shot over to Joel, but he was staring around like everyone else. I forced myself to slow my breathing down.

"Very well." Mr. Winston straightened up. "Would Hailey Kendrick and Tristan Johl please come forward?"

I felt everyone in the room swivel around to look at Tristan and me. I wanted to sink into the bench. Kelsie was staring at me with her mouth open. The link between my brain and my legs didn't seem to be working, and I didn't think I could stand. Tristan was standing, but looked confused.

"Ms. Kendrick. Front and center, please," Mr. Winston bellowed.

Tristan came to the end of the row and held out his hand for me.

"Don't worry. We didn't do anything," Tristan said softly in my ear.

I wanted to explain to him that it was complicated, that I had done something, but I couldn't get my mouth to form words. Everyone was watching us, and Mr. Winston was standing at the front like an executioner. I was shaking, but I managed to stand, and we walked to the front. There was a rustle of whispering. I would have turned and run out of the hall, but there was nowhere for me to go. You can't really run away in rural Vermont unless you have your own car.

"Mr. Winston, I'm sure there's been some sort of mistake," Tristan said, turning on the charm.

"Really?" Mr. Winston looked down his nose at Tristan. It was well known that Mr. Winston preferred the kids who came from "old money." He thought kids who were connected to Hollywood were trouble. He seemed almost happy to have finally caught one doing something wrong. "The both of you should know you could be expelled for this prank. Ms. Kendrick, I am especially disappointed in you. I expected far more from you as a member of the student council and a leader in this school. What do you have to say for yourself?"

I stared into his eyes. My mind seemed to have lost the ability to communicate.

"We had nothing to do with this," Tristan said, motioning to the severed arm that Mr. Hanson was still holding.

"I saw you," one of the security guards said as he stepped forward. "I heard something, just after eleven and when I got to the statue, I saw the arm on the ground and you standing there making out. I looked you straight in the face," he said, looking at me. He crossed his arms over his chest.

"But I was in study group," Tristan said, sounding lost.

"Then, who were you with?" Mr. Winston asked, turning to me. I could hear someone in the audience gasp.

"You were with some other guy?" Tristan asked. He looked as if I had slapped him.

"Tell me who else was involved," Mr. Winston demanded.

Out of the corner of my eye I saw Joel starting to stand. The situation was going from bad to worse. If Joel admitted that he was the person I'd been making out with during the Great Statue Destruction, then Tristan was going to be completely crushed. He already looked at if someone had scooped his guts out with a rusty ice cream scoop. If he heard in front of the entire school that it had been Joel I was kissing, he wouldn't be able to cope.

"It was some guy from town," I spit out. "I was with this guy, and we broke the statue as a joke."

"This is true?" Tristan's voice cracked. We were close enough that I could see his lower lip starting to shake. His eyes looked like he was close to crying. He would be gutted if he cried in front of everyone. He didn't even cry sophomore year when he broke his arm in gym class. I felt my face turn red hot with shame. Everyone in the crowd was staring at me like I had grown a tail. Even Mr. Winston looked unsettled. He had thought he had everything tied up, but things were turning out to be more complicated. The chapel bells on campus chimed eight. Mr. Winston glanced down at his watch, annoyed that even time was getting away from him.

"The rest of you are dismissed for classes. Ms. Kendrick, you'll come with me to the office." He took me by the elbow and guided me toward the door. "Mr. Johl, there's no need to stand there. You're going to be late." We brushed past Tristan. I could feel his eyes burning into my back as the dean and I walked out of the hall.

Fifteen minutes before, I had been sure that everything was going back to normal. Now my entire world had blown up and was never going to be the same.

9

I shifted on the wooden bench. It must have been made out of some type of especially hard wood designed to make people feel pain. I was stuck waiting outside Dean Winston's office in the area that held his secretary, while he spoke to my dad on the phone. Mr. Winston and I had already discussed:

- How what I'd done was vile and on par with kicking disabled kittens.
- That I was on the path to becoming a criminal and likely would spend the rest of my life in jail giving myself homemade tattoos with a needle and a Bic pen.
- That the statue was a work of art, and would I dare to tear the arm off the Mona Lisa? He didn't think so.

- That I was a disappointment to him, my family, my boyfriend, my fellow students, and likely all of Western civilization.

I watched out the window as people walked past. I wanted to see Tristan to explain, but at the same time I had no idea what I would say. How do you tell your boyfriend that you kissed someone else but you hadn't meant to? Kissing isn't exactly a common accident. I couldn't explain it to myself, so how was I going to explain it to him? I jumped, suddenly noticing Kelsie standing outside looking in. She met my eyes and spread her hands in a universal *WTF?* gesture. I shrugged, and for the first time felt like crying.

"Ms. Kendrick," Dean Winston barked. I spun around. He was standing in his doorway. "Your father would like to speak with you." He held the door open so I could walk past him into the office. His large desk was clean, with only the phone in the center of the highly glossed mahogany space. The red light blinked, indicating the speaker phone was on. Mr. Winston dropped into his leather chair and pointed to the small wooden chair across from him. I had hoped I might be able to talk to my dad by myself, but it looked like Winston was planning to have a front row seat for the discussion.

"Hi, Dad," I said, weaving my fingers together to avoid picking at my fingernails.

"Hailey, can you explain what's happened?" My dad's voice sounded clipped through the speaker.

"It was sort of a joke." My eyes darted over to Dean Winston, and I rushed to finish. "I realize it was a huge mistake and not remotely funny at all. It was one of those things that sort of just happened."

"Things like this don't just happen," my dad said. "This is very serious. If the school wanted to file charges for vandalism, they could. The cost of the statue is significant."

Out of the corner of my eye I could see Mr. Winston nodding along with what my dad was saying. He was most likely wishing my dad would come up with some form of vile punishment, but once your family sends you off to boarding school, there isn't that much more they can do to you.

"I'll pay for it. I can use some of the money in my savings account, and I'll get a job this summer and send the money here," I offered.

"You better believe you're going to pay for it, and you're also going to write the school administration an apology letter." A tired sigh came through the speaker. I could picture my dad at work in his office, rubbing his temples. Discipline wasn't really his thing. My mom used to do it, and after she died, he hadn't needed to punish me. I had been too busy being the perfect kid. We were in uncharted territory.

"There is one other issue still on the table," Dean Winston said, leaning over so his voice would be picked up by the speaker. He was stroking his tie as if it were a cat. The whole thing gave me the creeps, and I had to fight the urge to pull my chair farther away from him. "Hailey has not been willing to give us the name of the"—he cleared his throat—"young man from town that she was with last evening. "

"I don't see why his name matters," I said. "It was just a guy from town."

"I'm sure your father would also like to know about this *guy* from town that his daughter is cavorting about with in the middle of the night, committing acts of vandalism."

"I thought you were dating Taylor. Who is this boy?" My dad asked.

"Tristan. His name isn't Taylor. This was just a guy I met. I really don't want to talk about my dating life," I said.

"This boy is responsible for half the cost of the damages. Non-students are not allowed on school grounds after hours."

"I said I would pay for it," I said again, kissing my hefty savings account good-bye.

"Are you protecting this boy for some reason?" My dad asked. "Is he threatening you? How do we even know Hailey had anything to do with this vandalism? My daughter is not the type to be in trouble. I think it is far more likely that this boy was the instigator."

"Your daughter appeared to our security guard to be a very willing participant."

"What exactly are you trying to say about my daughter? I would think there might be a need to spend less time smearing her reputation and instead looking into how this boy was allowed on what is supposed to be a secure campus," my dad snapped back.

I ground down a millimeter of tooth enamel. I hated how both Dean Winston and my dad were talking about me like I wasn't even in the room. It seemed to me that it wasn't about the statue anymore. Now it was about which one of them was more in charge.

"This guy has nothing to do with this. I was the one who was upset. It was my idea to damage the statue. The guy was just there. Nothing more," I blurted out, shutting both of them up for a beat.

"Hail, why were you so upset?" My dad asked, his voice tuning in to what I was saying for the first time. I felt my throat seize shut with rage. He wanted to know why I was upset? Either he'd completely forgotten that he'd torpedoed our summer plans a day before, or it had mattered so little to him that he couldn't even imagine that I might have been upset about it. I pressed my lips together to hold in what words might come flying out. I felt myself starting to tear up, and I stared down into my lap.

"Mood changes can be a sign of substance use," Mr. Winston said. "If Hailey has fallen in with an unsavory crowd, this might be something we need to investigate."

Dean Winston was about to see a mood change. I pictured how satisfying it would be to sweep my arm across his desk and send the phone flying to the floor. I forced myself to take a deep breath.

"I'm not on drugs. I understand you want to know who I was with, but I'm not willing to get anyone else in trouble for something that was my fault. I'm not going to tell you. I'm not going to tell anyone."

"It's not that simple, Hailey. What happened impacts the safety of the entire school," Dean Winston said. "As you know, we've had security challenges of late with the paparazzi. If there are unauthorized people sneaking onto campus, we need to know."

"If she refuses to tell, I'm not certain what you expect to happen," my dad said. "We can't force her."

"I assure you, Mr. Kendrick, I have extensive experience working with teens. When direct requests are met with resistance, then we take further action. Your daughter will be placed on campus restriction. This means she will not be allowed off campus for any activity. No trips to the mall, no movies, no sporting events. She's not allowed to go down to the store to pick up soda, candy, or those fashion magazines they all seem to love. She isn't allowed to leave the campus grounds without an escort from the faculty until she decides to share with us the identity of who she was with last evening."

What Dean Winston seemed to have forgotten in coming up with a plan that he clearly thought would crush me, is that it wasn't like anyone was going to want to hang out with me. I had to cancel the biggest social event of the year, thanks to my dad, and I'd publically hurt the most popular guy on campus.

It wasn't like my boyfriend was going to want to take me anywhere. I couldn't imagine what Tristan thought of me. I could pretty much guess that this morning's assembly had dropped the whole nearly-naked Mandy scandal off the chart. Being stuck in my room by myself actually seemed like a gift rather than a punishment.

"That's fine," I said.

"While it might be fine for you, Ms. Kendrick, I doubt your classmates will share your perspective." Dean Winston leaned back in his chair, crossing his arms. "The entire campus will share your punishment."

I sat straight up. "You can't punish everyone. That's not fair."

"Evesham prides itself on its sense of community. It's been my experience that the pressure from one's peers is more convincing than anything I can do. If I can't persuade you to provide the name of the other person involved, then perhaps a week of no one being able to leave campus will be all the encouragement you need."

Winston looked really proud of himself. He seemed to be getting some kind of perverse pleasure out of the idea of seeing me ostracized by everyone I knew. I was starting to get the sense that he would see waterboarding as an acceptable form of information gathering too.

"Hailey, you should expect a punishment from me as well. We'll discuss it this weekend after you've had a chance to think about what you've done," my dad said. He might have wanted

Dean Winston to think he was giving me time to stew, but I suspected the truth was that my dad had no idea what to do in terms of a punishment and couldn't be bothered to take more time away from his job to deal with me. I hadn't given him a lot of practice over the past few years. The worst thing I'd done since my mom had died was forgetting to put the tub of ice cream back in the freezer, resulting in a puddle of French vanilla on his polished marble counter. Destruction of school property was a pretty big step up.

"That's not all," Dean Winston said, interrupting my dad before we could end this call from hell. "We expect Hailey to make reparations as to the cost of the statue, of course. However, we feel that true reparations are more than just taking money out of an account. Many of our students come from fortunate backgrounds, and as a result, coming up with funds often isn't an issue and not a large deterrent."

"What is it you're thinking of?" My dad cut him off before Dean Winston could go ahead and call me a spoiled brat, which is what he was hinting at.

"Hard work. Hailey will be assigned to work with the cleaning crew. Her hours will be tracked and those minimum wage earnings applied to repay the statue."

"You want me to be a janitor?" I had an image of myself in a gray jumpsuit with my name stitched over the pocket and the stench of Lysol following me around like a yellow cloud. After canceling my summer party, cheating on the most popular guy on campus, and getting everyone in the whole school on restriction, being one of the cleaning crew was really going to be the icing on the cake of my newfound leper status.

"When you make a mess, it's important to clean it up," Dean Winston said.

"I agree," my dad said.

"What about school? I have college apps to finish." It wasn't that I thought I was above cleaning, but in the big scheme of things, was it more important for me to scrape gum off the bottom of desks or focus on pulling up my grade in history so I could go to Yale? Seriously, this couldn't get any worse.

"We're hardly planning to make you work around the clock." Dean Winston looked over my shoulder and nodded at someone behind me, before turning his attention back to my dad and me. "But you will be monitored, of course. I've selected a student leader to keep an eye on your participation and encourage you to do the right thing regarding being fully honest about this situation."

I couldn't wait to see who was going to be Winston's lackey. I turned around and saw Joel in the doorway. When he saw me, his face went white. He'd overheard what Winston had said and knew he was my new jailer.

I was wrong. Winston had found a way to make things worse.

10

I needed to be alone or I was going to lose it. I wasn't sure what losing it was going to look like, but I was willing to bet it would make what had happened with the statue look like small-time. I pictured myself standing in the center of the quad screaming and flopping around on the ground like a two-year-old having a full-on meltdown.

When Winston finally dismissed me, I put my head down and hustled toward my room. I was supposed to go to the last ten minutes of calculus, but whatever. I needed at least ten minutes of silence where I could just sit and pull things together. Everything had blown apart. I felt like I was standing in the middle of the rubble of my life, unsure about what to pick up. My hands wouldn't stop shaking, and it felt like I could throw up at any second. However, I couldn't be alone, because I had Joel stuck to my side like Velcro, and he was following me back to the dorms.

Joel shuffled through the leaves. "What should we do?"

This was the fourth time Joel had asked this question since we'd walked out of Winston's office.

"I don't know. Nothing, I guess." I wondered if people looking out of the classroom windows were watching, and what they thought of me. I couldn't look Joel in the face. I still wasn't sure how to handle what had happened. My plan of ignoring it altogether was now going to be a bit harder, since the entire school knew there'd been a kiss, even if they didn't know who it had been with.

"Do you want me to confess?" Joel asked. "I was going to, right after the meeting. I followed Tristan out of the hall, but then he puked."

I stopped short. "What?"

"He threw up. I've never seen him like that. I was going to tell him that it was me, that I was the one who kissed you, but when I saw him, I couldn't."

I couldn't think about Tristan now. I forced the image of him out of my mind. Tristan acted cool and aloof about everything, but he wasn't. He was used to protecting himself. It came from years of having photographers following him around hoping to capture a vulnerable moment. I remembered him telling me that when he was six, he took a nasty spill off of his bike. His knee had a huge gash, and there was a flap of skin, a triangle of flesh, that was ripped free and hanging. Tristan said it was that flap of skin that had really freaked him out, almost more than the pain.

He'd been afraid that if he'd pulled on it, his entire skin would have peeled off his body. He'd started crying, and someone had snapped a picture just as his mom had come rushing up to his side. The picture ended up on the cover of some tabloid magazine, and the kids he went to school with teased him about being a crybaby. He told me that was the last time he ever cried in public. I couldn't imagine what he must have been feeling to be upset enough to puke in the bushes.

"I could get kicked out of school for this," Joel said, snapping my attention back. "I'll lose my scholarship for sure."

"You're not going to get kicked out," I countered, continuing toward my dorm.

"Winston is just big enough of an ass to do it. All the shit he's doing with you, putting the whole school on restriction, the cleaning crew detail, that's all because he can. He loves a power trip. He'd like nothing better than to put someone like me back in my place. He doesn't think I belong here, and certainly not in the Ivy Leagues. People like me are supposed to clean his house and wash his car."

"You're not going to get kicked out, because I'm not going to say anything."

"I can't let you take the heat for this on your own."

"It'll blow over. He can't keep the entire school on lockdown forever. Someone will whine to their parents, who will threaten to pull their donation for a new wing on the science building, and that will be the end of it. We've just got to wait it out." I stopped at the stoop to my dorm and fumbled for my key card.

"Are you sure?"

I wanted to yell in his face that of course I wasn't sure. I'd never been in trouble like this before. How was I supposed to make him feel better when I felt like shit? I spun around to say something, but stopped short. Joel was still pale, and his hands were jammed deep into his pockets. He was scared.

I put my hand on his shoulder and managed what I hoped was a reassuring smile. "It'll be okay."

"I'm sorry I'm the one monitoring your punishment." Joel kicked the stair halfheartedly, unable to meet my eyes.

"I'm not sorry. I'd rather have you do it than someone else. Can you imagine if he'd put Mandy in charge? She'd love to see me tarred and feathered."

Joel laughed. It sounded a bit forced. "When she realizes that you're standing between her and her regular trips to Starbucks, I think she'll demand we bring back burning at the stake."

"I forgot about her caramel macchiato addiction. I bet she ends up with the shakes before the day is over." I gave his shoulder a pat. "That almost makes it worth it."

"You should go. It's one thing to miss the rest of calculus, but you need to be on time for history."

My stomach sank to a new low. Any chance of Ms. Brown giving me a pass on turning in our project on time had disappeared. "So, what happens if I'm late, you'll give me a demerit?"

Joel looked up, his eyebrows squishing together with concern. "I'd *have* to give you a demerit. He's going to be watching me, making sure I enforce everything. It's not that I'd want to, but I can't afford to cut you any slack. He'll say I'm not living up to my role as president."

My hand dropped from his shoulder, and a lump formed in my throat. I hadn't felt this alone since my dad had dropped me off at Evesham for the first time. "I know. I should go. I don't want to be late." I ran up the stairs without looking back.

11

I lay on my bed, staring up at the ceiling. I had less than fifteen minutes to get to history. I wondered if this was how people felt after some kind of disaster, like an earthquake or a plane crash. The last time I'd felt like this was after my mom died. My grandma had taken me to the mall to get black dress shoes for the funeral. The mall was full of people bustling around, swinging shopping bags to the bouncy beat of the pop music that pumped through the speakers. The smells of pizza and fresh baked cookies competed as they poured out of the food court. It seemed like everyone was wearing artificially bright colors, like a clown academy had run amok in the hallway.

I'd stopped in the doorway of the mall, and a salesclerk from the nearby department store had seen me hesitate, and had moved in to spray me with a puff of perfume. She'd blathered about how there was a sale and if I bought the perfume I could get a free lipstick. I'd taken the flyer she pressed into my hand and looked down at it, trying to make sense of what was written on it, but it looked like Arabic. My grandmother took me by the elbow and guided me through the crowd to the shoe store. I felt like I was watching myself, or someone playing me, on TV. It didn't seem it was possible that this was reality. How could everything be going on just the same when my world had stopped? My mom was dead, but to everyone else it was just another day at the mall. They were complaining about jeans that didn't fit, and whispering about boys who were hanging out at the arcade. The salesclerks just wanted another sale or for their shifts to end, and little kids were still tossing pennies into the fountain and making wishes. I remember feeling how small and insignificant my life must have been, that when it came crashing down, it wasn't enough to make a ripple in the rest of the world.

Now it was happening all over again. I had lost Tristan. I was sure of it. He had been one of the constants in my life since moving to Evesham. We went everywhere together. People thought of us as one unit, Tristan and Hailey. His popularity had rubbed off on me. People liked me because Tristan did. They worried about what I thought and copied my hairstyles. I was pretty and smart, but Tristan had been what had made me special. He would never forgive me for what had happened, and I couldn't even explain it to him without hurting him even more.

I rolled into a ball on the bed. By now the announcement would have been made in classes that everyone was on restriction.

Anyone who had thought it was sort of cool that Miss Perfect Kendrick had destroyed the school statue would suddenly be changing their minds. Now my prank was going to cost them their freedom, and that wasn't going to be appreciated. Not at all.

I didn't want to run away. That would mean starting all over someplace else. What I wanted to do was disappear, but that wasn't an option. Neither was turning back time and not getting myself into this situation at all. What had I been thinking? Just like when my mom died, there was no way to change what had happened. I had to get through it. If I got through that, I could get through this. I would do it exactly the same way. I would put my head down and toe the line. I had gotten all wild and crazy for one night, and look where it had gotten me. I was going to follow every rule, guideline, and bylaw. I was going to follow rules that hadn't even been made yet. I was going to be so good I would make Mother Teresa look like an escapee from a *Girls Gone Wild* video. I wasn't sure how I was going to make this up to everyone, but I was willing to try.

12

When I walked into history, everyone stopped talking and turned to face me. I ducked my head and slid into my seat next to Kelsie. She had her book open and was pretending to be riveted by the description of the battle of Saratoga. I slid my foot across the aisle and lightly tapped her leg.

"Hey," I whispered. She looked over, and I saw she was ticked. Not just a little angry but seriously pissed off. I pulled my leg back, my face no doubt registering the shock. I hadn't thought she would be one of the people who would be mad.

Kelsie leaned over so that no one could overhear us. "I thought we were friends," she hissed.

"We are," I said.

Kelsie shook her head like she couldn't believe a word that came out of my mouth. "Really? Because I would think that if we were friends, you might have thought it was important to share something like that with me. I don't know. I thought friends told each other stuff. What the hell do I know?" She turned back around and stuffed her nose back in her book.

I slunk down in my seat and did my best to ignore the whispering around me. Ms. Brown walked in and perched on the edge of her desk. She was thin and angular, with a long nose. She reminded me of a heron waiting to pounce. Her gaze swept across the room. She paused at my desk and raised one pencil thin eyebrow in my direction. I could feel her disappointment coming off in waves.

"Hailey, would you and Kelsie like to present first?"

I stood up next to my desk. "Our presentation isn't done. It's my fault. Kelsie finished yesterday, and I said I would get my half done last night, but I didn't." I sat back down, my cheeks burning.

"That's unfortunate. I would ask what was important enough to keep you from your studies, but I trust we've already discussed that topic enough this morning," she said.

Someone in the back of the room giggled, but the sound was choked off when Ms. Brown looked over. I could feel Kelsie eyeing me, evaluating what I'd said and deciding if she would say anything or keep quiet. It might as well have been completely my fault. If I hadn't screwed up last night, the project would be done and we'd be standing up there right now talking about the importance of the French to the success of the American Revolution.

"Very well. I'll expect you two to present tomorrow. We'll discuss the impact of this extension later." She looked down at her grade book. "Phillip, let's have you and your partner start us off."

When the bell rang for the end of class, I sat in my seat while everyone else streamed out of the room. The room was quiet except for the ticking of the clock on the back wall and the sound of Ms. Brown tapping her long fingernail on her desk.

"'Nothing is a greater stranger to my breast, or a sin that my soul more abhors, than that black and detestable one, ingratitude,'" she said.

My forehead scrunched up. I had no idea what she was talking about.

"It's a quote from George Washington during the war," she clarified.

"Oh." I pulled my notebooks together. I didn't know if she was calling me an ingrate, or was implying that Kelsie should be grateful that I was taking the blame for our project, or was randomly spitting out historical quotes. History teachers are an odd breed. Maybe it comes from inhaling all those dusty books. "I'll make sure our presentation is done by tomorrow."

"It's an automatic reduction in your grade."

"I know."

She waited until I was almost out the door. "If you're interested, I may have some extra credit assignments you could do.

It might balance out your overall grade. The assignments are of course also open to Kelsie if she wishes."

A smile spread across my face and I gave her a nod. The brief upswing in my mood lasted until I got out into the hallway. Kelsie was leaning against the wall waiting for me.

"I have no idea what you're trying to pull," she said, her jaw thrust forward.

"Nothing. The project is my fault. I should have finished it. It was just, with everything that happened, I honestly forgot."

Kelsie sighed. "What kind of sign of the apocalypse is it when Hailey Kendrick forgets to do homework?" She looked around the hall to make sure we were alone. "Who were you with last night, and why the hell did you cut the arm off the statue?"

"We didn't cut it off. It sort of fell off. Not by accident or anything. I was sitting on it. We were trying to get his head off, actually."

Kelsie looked at me like I was speaking another language. "How long have you been cheating on Tristan?"

"I'm not cheating on Tristan," I said firmly. "There wasn't any big secret Romeo and Juliet relationship. It was a onetime kiss. It shouldn't have happened. It was a heat-of-the-moment kind of thing. A bunch of stuff went wrong yesterday, there was the project to finish, and then I got nail polish all over my mom's sweatshirt. Then the thing with my dad . . ." My voice trailed off. "I had to get out of my room and blow off some steam. I was so mad—mad at everything. Then there was the statue, and I happened to meet this guy there, and stuff happened." I shrugged. I knew it sounded crazy. It was crazy, but it was the truth and the only explanation I had.

"What's some townie doing on campus?" Kelsie's nose wrinkled up a bit when she said "townie," as if I had been caught kissing a homeless guy who smelled like cat pee.

"He was taking a walk and ended up on campus. No big deal. There wasn't a big plot or plan. The whole thing was like a weird freak accident. It just happened. You know me. You know this isn't the kind of thing I do."

"Man, when you decide to blow off steam, you sure do it big. Most people just sneak a few beers and throw up."

Throwing up reminded me of Tristan and what Joel had seen. "I have to talk to Tristan," I said.

Kelsie grabbed my hand. "No, you shouldn't. He's really hurt. And ticked."

"I have to tell him my side of things. What if he thinks I've been cheating on him?"

"You did cheat on him. You were making out with some guy. The security guard saw you."

"We weren't making out. It was one kiss. One kiss by accident." Why was that so hard to grasp? "I don't want Tristan thinking that I've been sneaking around behind his back. I feel sick about what happened, Kels. If I could change it, I would, but all I can do is tell him how sorry I am."

"Leave it to me," she said.

"What?"

"Trust me. I talked to Tristan right after the assembly. He's not interested in talking to you right now." She waved her hand in front of my face to stop me from saying anything. "I'll talk to him for you. Try to smooth things over. He's really hurt, and he doesn't want you to see that. You know how he is."

I nodded, chewing on my lower lip. I wanted a chance to explain, but it was quite likely he wasn't interested in talking to me. It might be easier if she talked to him first, gave him a chance to calm down. "Would you do that for me? Explain how I feel terrible, and that it was just a onetime thing."

"I'll talk to him. You might want me to talk to a few other people too. Everybody's pretty ticked about the restriction thing."

"Did you hear what else? Winston put me on janitorial duty."

"Gross. Why?"

"I'm supposed to be learning the importance of cleaning up my own messes."

"I'd have my parents complain."

"My dad thinks it's a great idea. He's still coming up with a punishment of his own."

Kelsie shook her head sadly. "This situation is totally screwed."

I wanted to throw my arms around Kelsie. It felt so good to talk to a friend, to feel like at least one person was on my side. "Thanks for talking to Tristan. It means a lot to me."

Kelsie hitched her backpack up onto her shoulder. The bell was ringing to let us know there were only three minutes left. "Don't thank me yet. I'll talk to him, but I'm not sure it's going to do any good."

13

When I was a really little kid, I wanted to be invisible. I used to pretend that I had a magic cape that would make me disappear. I loved the idea of slipping in and around what was happening in the world and no one even knowing I was there. I would tie a pillowcase around my neck and slink around the house. My parents would play along, saying in loud voices: "Where has Hailey gotten off to? I don't see her anywhere." Then I would cover my mouth and giggle. Forget flying, or setting fires with my mind—I was convinced being invisible would be the best superpower ever.

Turns out being invisible sucks.

I used to say being popular wasn't important to me. That was before I found out what it was like to be on the other side. Now I realized that being popular had come with significant advantages. The week dragged on—snide comments in the hallways, my toothbrush knocked off the countertop onto the bathroom floor, no one saving me a seat in class or complimenting me on what I was wearing. The bubble of approval that used to surround me, people telling me how great I looked, laughing at my jokes, and agreeing with my views, was busted. What I noticed the most about my new status was how lonely I felt. I realized that before, I had almost never been alone. There was always someone calling out to me when I walked across campus, or stopping by my room to chat, or asking me for advice. If I went out, there was always someone who wanted to come along or a group that would beg me to join them. Now no one wanted me around.

I had never been so glad to see the weekend. All I wanted to do was hole up in my dorm room and pull my covers up over my head; instead I was following Joel to the administration building to begin the next stage of my humiliation.

Parked in front of the building was a beat-up red pickup truck. It looked like the only thing holding it together was the random bumper stickers that were plastered all over it. I'D RATHER BE SKIING. ADRENALINE IS MY DRUG OF CHOICE. FRODO FAILED. ELVIS HAS LEFT THE PLANET. There was dried mud sprayed across the side panels. A guy leaned against the truck reading a paperback. He was tall, at least six feet, with long hair that he had tied back in a ponytail. He seemed to be around my age, maybe a bit older. He looked like a surfer who had gotten very lost coming back from the beach and had somehow ended up in Vermont. When the guy saw us walking up, he carefully folded over the page he was reading, to mark his spot, and tossed the book into his truck.

"You must be Joel," the guy said. He turned to me with a half smile. "And you must be the guilty party coming to scrub your soul and the toilets clean."

I didn't say anything to him, but pleaded with Joel. "I don't see why I can't be assigned a project to do on my own. I could paint a classroom or something."

"That doesn't sound like a team player attitude," the guy said. "You know what they say: Many hands make light work."

Great. I was partnered up with a motivational speaker who smelled like Mr. Clean.

"Dean Winston wants you to work on the cleaning crew, not on your own," Joel said. "This is Drew. He'll show you around and make sure you know what needs to get done." Joel stood there looking at both of us, his face pinched. "Are you going to be okay?"

"Don't worry. She's going to be washing floors, not defusing bombs in a war zone." Drew clapped Joel on the shoulder and started walking, indicating I should follow him. I didn't.

Joel waited until Drew had taken a few steps away. "You know if I could take your place I would. I hate to see you having to do this."

I wasn't sure how it had ended up that I had to be the one to comfort Joel when he was going to be able to go back to bed and I was going to be the one cleaning fly corpses out of the lamps.

"It'll be okay. Cleaning is good exercise. It's like a step class, only more productive." Joel squeezed my hand and then left, looking as if he were dropping me off at the executioner.

A disbelieving snort came from behind me. I spun and saw Drew standing there next to a cleaning cart. He rolled it over to me. "Do you want to push the cart? Really feel the calorie burn?"

I pressed my lips into a thin tight line and yanked the cart over. I must have pulled too hard, because the mop flew off and the handle smacked me right between the eyes. Drew gave another snort as he choked back a laugh.

"Do you think that's funny? If that had bleach on it, I could be blind."

"You look okay, Helen Keller. I'm guessing it takes more to keep you down than you think. Let's get going before you amputate a finger with the dustpan. It's got that sharp edge, you know. Careful. There's a feather duster, too. It might be full of bird flu germs."

I shoved the giant Rubbermaid cart ahead of me and walked away before he could make fun of me anymore. One wheel was stuck and wouldn't turn, so I wasn't able to make the dramatic exit I had been hoping for.

I rolled the cart into the first classroom and looked around, wondering where we were supposed to start.

"We need to wash all the desks down with disinfectant, mop the floors, wash the windows, and give everything else a quick wipe down. You do know how to clean, don't you, Prima

Donna? I'm hoping you learned something watching your maid all those years."

I didn't dignify his comment with an answer. It was true I had always had a maid, but it had never struck me as a job that required a lot of experience. I was pretty sure I could figure it out.

Drew bent over and started to pull various bottles and rags out of the cart. "You can pick what you want to tackle. The desks are easy. You might want to start with that and work up to the hard stuff." He looked up at me, and when I didn't comment, he tossed a rag and a can in my direction.

I looked at the can. It was some kind of industrial cleaner, most likely able to eat my flesh off if I got it on my skin. It looked way less user friendly than the organic, good-for-the-environment cleaner that my dad's cleaning service uses. I flipped the can over so I could see the warning label.

"Have you had any formal training for this job?" I asked Drew.

He looked over the mop bucket at me. "How did you know I got my master's degree in this?"

"I'm being serious. You know if you mix some cleaning supplies you can create chlorine gas? It can kill people."

Drew smacked his forehead. "Ah, that explains what happened to everyone else. I thought the death toll was high for this job."

"Have you considered a career in stand-up? Your talents are clearly wasted here," I said. I sprayed the desk closest to me, inhaling the oily stink of the cleaner. I wiped it down and moved to the next.

"Don't worry, Prima Donna. If you start to look faint, I'll drag your body to safety."

"My name is Hailey."

"Okay, Hailey. I'll drag your prima-donna butt to safety, right after I finish my lunch break. Never underestimate the appeal of a leftover Spicy Italian from Subway."

I made a face at him. "Chlorine gas can cause brain damage too."

"You're going to want to make sure you wipe under the desktop as well. A lot of these classy kids drill their noses during class and leave boogers under there," he said, pointing.

"That's disgusting." I pulled my hands away from the desk. I sat in some of these chairs. It had never occurred to me to check underneath them.

"You're telling me. I'm not joking either. Look for yourself if you don't believe me. Some of the desks practically have snot stalactites growing down. You would think instead of a Mercedes they could have bought some manners."

I glanced at Drew as he mopped the floor. I'd met his type in town before. They resent us for who we are. It isn't our fault our parents have money. What did people expect us to do? Give it all away to charity? Did he think I believed for a moment that he would send it all to Afghanistan to build schools if the situation were reversed? Most likely he'd spend it on fast food and

NASCAR races. I wiped the desks with renewed vigor. The last thing I wanted Drew to do was whine that I didn't pull my weight. I really wished I had a pair of rubber gloves to wear, though. The idea of touching someone else's crusty snot grossed me out. Since I was on restriction, I couldn't buy any gloves in town, and I wasn't sure I could bring myself to ask Drew to do me any favors. Maybe I could buy a pair from someone who worked in the cafeteria.

"So, what did you do to land yourself here?" he asked as he moved the mop across the floor.

"What makes you think I did anything?"

Drew's lip raised on one side. "Of course. My mistake. How kind of you to volunteer your time. Or are you planning a career in the cleaning arts and looking to log some valuable practical experience?" He leaned on his mop. "Come on. Fess up. Did you get caught pawning someone's silver spoon right out of their mouth?"

"What is your issue with me?"

Drew laughed. "You should see yourself. Your face is all red."

"You like annoying people, don't you?"

"As you can tell, this job isn't exactly a huge intellectual drain. I have to do something else to keep myself entertained."

"I wouldn't think you would require much to keep you intellectually challenged. Walking and talking, for example."

"I'm remarkably skilled at multitasking, actually. Check this out." Drew grabbed a couple rolls of toilet paper off the cart and began to juggle them. Great. I was stuck working with Bozo the Cleaning Clown.

"You're impossible to insult."

"Years of practice. My ego is armor plated." He tossed the toilet rolls back into the cart and picked the mop back up. "Besides, I knew you'd insult me, so I was able to prepare. Your type never likes the help when we get uppity."

"My type? What exactly do you mean by that?"

"You shouldn't ask. The answer is just going to upset you. In my experience your type is overemotional. Sensitive."

"You think you know everything about me?"

"Not everything, but I'm betting I've got the big picture covered."

"You know what I did to land myself here? I was the one who broke the statue in the quad," I said, putting my hands on my hips. I felt almost proud of myself when I saw his surprise.

"You?"

"Yes, me. I guess you don't know my type as well as you thought."

Drew looked at me as if he were reappraising my character. "I guess not. My opinion of you has just gone up. I wouldn't have pegged you as the vandal rebel-without-a-cause type. Personally, I've always hated that statue. The knight always looks like he has a lance wedged up his ass. I'm impressed you did it. I would have thought you were a by-the-rules kind of person. You don't look like you would cross an empty street without being in an approved crosswalk with the light on your side."

I stopped short. "Crossing the street can be riskier than you think. It can change everything."

Drew tossed me a fresh roll of paper towels. "True. Thing is, Prima Donna, anything can be a game changer. The question is, why do you assume the change has to be bad?"

14

I sat up in bed, using my finger to hold my place in *The Count of Monte Cristo*. I thought I had heard something. I paused for a beat, but when I didn't hear anything else, I went back to Dantes's revenge plans. A door opened down the hall, and a burst of music shot into the hallway. I heard a bunch of girls giggle as they walked by. I waited to see if anyone would drop by my room, but they walked right past. There are few things sadder than doing homework on a Saturday night, not because you're behind but because you have nothing else to do. I opened the book again, but the words marched back and forth across the page without making any sense. I chucked the book to the floor.

This was stupid. I had friends. They weren't just Tristan's friends, but we were never going to be able to hang out as a group if I couldn't make things right with Tristan. He didn't have to forgive me and throw his arms around me, but we couldn't keep up the silent treatment. Every time I stumbled across Tristan, in the hallway for classes or in the dining hall, he would freeze. His entire body would go stiff as if he had been exposed to a nerve agent, and then he would turn away. I tried to smile or even say a quiet hello, but he looked straight past me as if I were invisible. It was time for me to talk to Tristan directly. Kelsie kept telling me to give him more time, but how was time going to help if it was time spent hating me? I looked over at my clock. There was an hour before the dorms were locked for the night. The one good thing about a school-wide restriction was that I knew where to find everyone.

I slipped across the quad into Tristan's dorm. The guys' dorm always smelled like a mix of Axe, sweat, and popcorn. In the front lobby there was a group playing some weird version of full contact soccer, where the sofa seemed to be one goal. There was no clear way to identify who was on what team, and a smaller group was trying to watch a sci-fi movie in the corner, while sitting on the same couch. Our dorm had Ms. Estes, but Tristan's was monitored by Mr. Harrington. Mr. Harrington had served in the military before becoming a dorm monitor. There was a theory that he had some kind of post-traumatic stress syndrome and as a result was on heavy medication that kept him mellow. He couldn't be bothered with enforcing the million small rules in the student guide. I guess if you were used to seeing people blowing themselves up trying to set roadside bombs, you couldn't get too worked up about some fifteen-year-old kid forgetting to tuck in his uniform shirt. I wished I could live there. It was still a dorm, but it felt more like a home.

Tristan and Joel's room was on the second floor. There was an open space near the top of the stairs that was supposed to be a public study area, but it had somehow morphed into being an extension of their room. Tristan had bought a big flat-screen TV that he'd plugged in out there, and no one turned it on without checking with him first. It was a strictly invitation-only public space. As I climbed the stairs, I could hear voices. It sounded like a decent-size crowd was hanging out. I could make out Joel and one of our friends, Aidan, debating if they wanted to order a pizza. They had the hockey game on. I'd practiced on the way over what I would do and say. Making a big deal out of it would only focus everyone on it, so my plan was to act casual. I took a deep breath and got ready to face Tristan.

"This is bogus. I had a date tonight," Aidan said. "Just because Hailey got lucky, I can't."

I froze in place. I peered around the corner. Kelsie was folded into the corner of the sofa, flipping through a magazine. Joel and Aidan were sharing the remainder of the sofa, and Tristan was sprawled on the floor. There were a couple of other guys watching the game, and two sophomore girls wearing way too much makeup were giggling like a broken record.

"Dream on. It's going to take a lot more than a movie and large popcorn to convince a girl to sleep with you," Joel said, chucking a throw pillow at his head.

"Hey, I was going to spring for the real butter for the popcorn. I was willing to spare no expense. I wasn't looking for a cheap lay, just an easy one."

"You guys are pigs," Kelsie said without looking up from her magazine.

"If you wanted an easy lay, you should have asked Hailey out," Tristan said. "If she'll do a townie, then I guess she'll do anyone."

My heart stopped beating. I couldn't believe he had just said that. Everyone looked embarrassed, but no one spoke up to defend me.

"I don't think it's fair that we all have to be on restriction just because of what she did," one of the sophomore girls said.

Kelsie whacked the girl on the back of the head with her magazine. "You should stay out of it. What do you care about restriction? You weren't going anyplace."

The sophomore blushed and looked down at her lap. I felt like pumping my fist in the air. *You tell that stupid lip-glossed silver-eye-shadowed freak, Kels!* That girl would have licked my shoes clean a week ago if I had asked her to. How dare she suddenly plop down in my group of friends and judge me.

"I still can't believe . . ." Tristan's voice trailed off. His jaw thrust forward, and I knew that meant he was fighting back tears. Suddenly I forgave him for what he'd said. He was hurt and was trying to lash out. I wanted to rush into the room and throw my arms around him and tell him that everything would be okay and that we could work through this.

Kelsie leaned over and gently laid her hand on the side of Tristan's face. He pressed his hand to hers and closed his eyes. It felt like a knife sliding between my ribs to stab my heart. I knew she was just trying to comfort him, but it felt too intimate, too personal. Then I hated myself for thinking anything bad about Kelsie, when she was the only one who had stood up for me since everything had happened.

I didn't want to be there anymore. There was no way I could sit down and act like things were going to be okay. I needed to get out of there. I took a step back and stepped into nothingness.

My arms spun around trying to regain my balance. I must have been closer to the top of the stairs than I'd thought. For a split second I thought I was going to be okay, but then my ankle rolled to the side and I fell.

I screamed as I bounced down the stairs. I rolled down like a tumbleweed, my feet slamming against the wall as I went. I saw flashes of red carpet runner as I spun, and I prayed that I wouldn't break anything.

When I finally hit the bottom of the stairs, my head was throbbing and I had torn a hole in my yoga pants. I could hear people rushing to see what had happened. I tried to sit up, and winced when I put my hand on the floor to prop myself up. It felt like I must have sprained my wrist. In addition to the two nails I had broken cleaning classrooms today, now my pinky nail was sheared off and bleeding. I heard someone gasp, and I looked up. At the top of the stairs Tristan, Joel, and Kelsie were looking down at me.

"Ms. Kendrick," a voice said. I spun around to see Mr. Harrington standing in the lobby. "How nice of you to drop by."

15

Mr. Harrington helped me to my feet. I was shaking from the shot of adrenaline. Everything hurt. It felt like I had been run over by a truck, but I was pretty sure no permanent damage had been done. I looked over each of my limbs. The crowd of soccer players from the lobby was jockeying for position. They seemed disappointed that I didn't appear to have broken anything, my brain wasn't leaking out my ears, and my shirt hadn't popped off. They would have been happy with either guts or boobs, but this wasn't as interesting as they had hoped.

It is a truth universally acknowledged that if you do something embarrassing like fall down the stairs in front of a group of people, you are required to act like you are fine, even if you aren't. Your arm could have a bone jutting out, and you would still try to laugh it off as if everything were hunky dory. *This compound fracture? It's nothing! I like to let my bones out of my body once in a while for fresh air. It's good for them.*

"I'm fine," I said, trying to give Mr. Harrington the impression that nothing important had happened and he didn't need to call Ms. Estes. She played by the book. She would require me to go to the hospital to make sure I didn't have a brain bleed or anything that could be blamed on her. If there were painful medical tests I would have to undergo, she'd love it even more. With my luck she would insist on sleeping in my room so she could wake me up every ten minutes in case I had a concussion. I took a step back from Mr. Harrington so that he could see I wasn't going to fall over. He pulled a Kleenex from his pocket and handed it to me. He motioned with his hand to my mouth. I touched my lip with the Kleenex and saw a bright bloom of red appear. One of my teeth must have cut my lip. Great.

I looked back to the top of the stairs. Tristan was starting to back away. Joel's mouth was hanging open in shock. He couldn't have looked more surprised if he had found the tooth fairy lying sprawled at the bottom of his staircase. He looked down at me and then over at Tristan, as if he weren't sure what might happen.

"Tristan, wait." I started up the stairs after him, wincing and adding an ankle strain to the list of injuries. I slipped between Kelsie and Joel at the top.

"What are you doing here?" Kelsie whispered as I went past.

I didn't bother to answer. I kept my focus on Tristan, who was still walking away. The two sophomore girls were standing in the hall, thrilled to have a front row view of this action. I was surprised they didn't pull out popcorn and Team Tristan T-shirts.

"Stop." I grabbed the back of Tristan's sweater. He whirled around, and I took a quick step back.

"What do you want?" he asked in a hard, flat voice.

"I need to talk to you," I said.

Tristan laughed, and the sound was harsh, nearly barking. "You know what I need? I need to know that I can trust the people in my life. I need to know my girlfriend of four years hasn't been screwing around on me. I need to know when someone is talking to me that they're telling me the truth."

"I'll tell you the truth."

"Who was the guy?"

"I can't tell you that."

Tristan shook his head, crossing his arms in front of his chest. "Well, that's great. This has been a really useful conversation."

"That's not what's important. It doesn't matter who it was. What matters is that it didn't mean anything. It never should have happened, and if I could take it back, I would. I can tell you that it never happened before that night and it wouldn't have happened if I hadn't been in some sort of crazy state." I whirled my hands around my head to indicate just how nuts I was.

"How do you live with knowing what you did? I would never have done something like that to you. Never."

I looked down at my feet. He was right. He wouldn't have. Given the circles his parents traveled in and the fact that he was both good-looking and rich, Tristan was always surrounded by girls who wanted him. They'd flirt with him when I was standing right there, and he always brushed them off. He wasn't someone who didn't have opportunity; he was someone who didn't have that kind of motivation.

"I am so sorry. I'm more sorry than I've ever been in my life. I don't mind being on restriction and having to clean the school. I can even live with the fact that everyone's mad at me, but I hate that I hurt you."

"Do you love this guy?"

"No! He means nothing. The kiss meant nothing."

Tristan looked me straight in the eyes, his stare pinning me to the ground. "That makes it worse, you know. I know you think that somehow it will make me feel better, but it doesn't. You threw away everything, and it wasn't even for someone who mattered."

Tristan turned and went into his room, shutting the door behind him. I turned and faced Joel and Kelsie, who were standing behind me.

"Wow. The guy didn't mean anything to you? That's good to know," Joel said.

I closed my eyes. I seemed to be incapable of making anything go right. "That's not what I meant. This is complicated."

"You don't owe me any explanations." He moved past me to join Tristan in their room.

"You have a wad of Kleenex stuck to your lip," Kelsie said,

breaking the silence. "What's stuck up Joel's ass with the whole thing? Why does he think he deserves a bio on the guy?"

I started to cry. I wasn't making a sound, but my shoulders were shaking from the sobs. Kelsie stepped in and hugged me, letting me bury my face in her hair. My ankle and wrist were throbbing with pain, and the metallic taste of blood filled my mouth.

"What are you staring at?" Kelsie said over my shoulder to the sophomore girls. "Get a life. Go do something else somewhere else."

I could hear the girls scuttle off, whispering as they went. They would spread the news of my graceful fall down the stairs and my fight with Tristan to the rest of the student body faster than any emergency broadcast system. With the way things were going for me, they would act it out so that everyone could have the full experience.

"I want to go home," I whispered.

"Let's go." Kelsie grabbed her *Vogue* off the sofa and started to lead me back to our dorm.

When I'd said "home" I hadn't meant the dorm. I'd meant someplace that didn't even exist anymore. The house I used to have with my mom and dad had been sold. My dad's apartment had never been home to me. He'd never asked me what I wanted. Instead he'd had a decorator design a room for me. It was purple. I hate purple. I was a guest. A guest who didn't even rank having the guest room to myself, since my dad kept his treadmill in there too, as if my room were more of a storage closet.

"This is a nightmare," I mumbled as we walked outside. It was raining, and the wind whipped the drops so that they felt like razors hitting my skin.

"I told you it wasn't a good idea to talk to Tristan. He's really upset."

"He's got you to comfort him, though." The words flew out of my mouth. Turns out I was still thinking about her hand on the side of his face.

Kelsie stopped and turned to face me. "What do you want? Yes, Tristan's my friend, and if I can help him feel better, then I'm going to try to do that. I'm the kind of person who tries to think of my friends, which is why I'm standing in the rain with you now instead of upstairs watching the rest of the hockey game. For someone who got caught kissing some random guy, you sound awfully judgmental."

My insides crumpled like a wet tissue. Now I was making the only person who was on my side turn against me.

"I'm sorry. I don't know what's wrong with me. Everything I do or say is exactly the wrong thing. From now on I'm going to listen to your advice. Just tell me how to get through this."

"It won't do much for the situation with Tristan, but things would go a lot easier all around if you would spill the identity of the guy. One week on restriction isn't that bad. It gives everyone a chance to chill out, but if this stretches into next week, you're going to see people getting ticked. You aren't doing yourself any favors."

"I can't tell. I know it doesn't make any sense, but I can't."

"I hope that whoever he is, he's worth it," Kelsie said.

There was no way to explain that keeping Joel out of trouble and not involving him in the situation with Tristan was the only decent thing to come out of the situation so far. That night scared me. Not because of what had happened but because I hadn't thought I was the kind of person who could do something like that. Doing this one thing right gave me the hope that I was still, somewhere deep down, a decent person.

"Any other advice?" I asked.

"Keep your head down and pray someone else screws up even bigger. Who knows, maybe someone will sell a full frontal naked photo of Mandy and people will find something else to talk about."

"Like her third nipple?" I joked.

Kelsie laughed. "You know what she says . . ."

"It's a MOLE," we screamed together, and for a second I felt just a little bit better.

16

I was determined to make my Sunday cleaning shift, if not enjoyable, at least more tolerable. Based on how things were going, I wouldn't be separated from this cleaning job anytime in the near future, so I figured I might as well get along with Drew. While I thought it was unfair of him to lump all of us Evesham kids together as rich brats, it wasn't surprising. We were a fortunate crowd. It was the kind of school where the student parking lot was full of Mercedes and BMWs, and on parents' weekend there was more than one limo parked outside.

The night before I'd even had an idea of how to do something nice for Drew. Maybe if I were nice to someone who annoyed me, the universe would see that I was trying to do the right thing.

We were scheduled to clean the gym, and I was hoping that if I showed him a different side of myself he might let me be the one to run the floor polisher rather than having to pick gum, or god knows what else, out from under the bleachers.

"Good morning!" I said in a positive singsong voice so he would know there were no hard feelings from yesterday.

"Hey," he said, and then he froze in place when he saw me. "What the heck happened to you?"

I touched my lower lip. My flight down the stairs last night had resulted in quite a few injuries. I was so covered in bruises that I looked like a cheetah, including a giant bruise on my temple that looked like I'd colored a dot on my face with a black marker. My cut lower lip had swollen overnight. It looked like what would happen if Angelina Jolie got her mouth stuck in a vacuum.

"This?" I shrugged, trying to turn the whole thing into a joke. "Bar fight."

Drew crossed the floor and gently cupped my chin, turning my face right and left so he could assess the damage. The skin on his hands felt rough, but also warm. "Did someone hit you?" His eyes pinned me into place. "That's never okay. If you need help, you can tell me."

"Are you going to beat someone up for me?" I pulled my chin back, even though I had liked it resting in his hands. It wasn't that I wanted him to touch me, but it felt nice to be touched by anyone, given my current leper status. "How gallant."

"I'm being serious. My sister's ex-boyfriend used to hit her. There's a women's group in town that can help."

"They can't help me." I held up my hand to deflect his argument. Who knew that in the chest of a teen janitor beat the heart of a knight in shining armor? It wasn't fair to compare him with Tristan or Joel, given the circumstances, but they had seen me fall and hadn't offered this much sympathy. "No one hit me. I fell down the stairs."

"Why did you fall down the stairs?"

"Well, it wasn't exactly a well-thought-out plan. It was an accident."

"You don't strike me as the klutzy type. Did something upset you?"

"What is this, the inquisition?" I laughed, but it sounded fake even to my own ears. "No big story. I was rushing around and missed the top step."

"All right." Drew looked around the gym. "You look pretty banged up. I'm not sure you should be going up and down the bleachers bending over to do gum detail. Try to take it easy."

"I could sit over there and supervise," I offered. "Keep you entertained with jokes or something."

"Nice try, Prima Donna, but the best thing when you've taken a fall is to keep moving. Otherwise your muscles stiffen up."

"So you have a lot of experience falling down stairs?"

"I usually manage stairs, but I've taken my fair share of falls. I like to ski and snowboard, and I've wiped out mountain climbing a couple of times."

"Mountain climbing?"

Drew laughed. "You should see your face. It's like I told you I like to swim in sewers."

"I don't see the point in climbing a mountain, just to say you did? It seems awfully risky."

"It's more than bragging rights. It's about pushing yourself. Challenging yourself to do more than you thought you could. Be all you can be kind of thing."

This was a great entry into what I wanted to talk about. I'd even stopped by the computer lab in our dorm to print out a few information sheets I'd found the night before. "It's interesting you bring up the idea of reaching for more." I motioned for Drew to sit down on the bench. "I hope you don't think I'm sticking my nose in where it doesn't belong."

"I find that people who start a conversation like that are just about to stick their nose in the wrong place. It's the same with people who say, 'I don't want to offend you, but . . .'"

I handed Drew the sheets of paper from my jacket pocket. He flipped through them and then looked over at me. "What's this?"

"You're really young, right? You're not that much older than me."

"I'm nineteen."

"There you go, nineteen. That's not too old."

"Too old for what?"

"You seem like you work really well with your hands and you're smart. There are a bunch of local programs where you could train to be an electrician or in another skilled trade."

Drew chuckled. "Wow. Is this your good deed for the day?"

"I'm not being rude. I'm actually trying to help. You act like everyone who has money thinks they're better than everyone else, and what I'm saying is that I think you can do better than what you're doing. I meant it as a compliment." It hadn't occurred to me that it would offend him. Wow. It seemed I could even screw up being nice to people.

"Well, then, I'll take it in the spirit you intended." Drew heaved himself off the bench and plugged in the floor polisher. "Since we're passing around advice, do you mind if I give you some?"

I could tell I wasn't going to like anything he said, but I couldn't very well refuse. "Are you going to tell me to keep my nose out of things?"

"Nope. One of the problems in the world is that people aren't willing to stick their noses in more often. We all ought to look out for each other better. My advice is for you to loosen up a little. For someone who has the whole world on a silver platter, you're wound way too tight."

"I don't have the world on a platter."

"Fine. For someone who has the world on a salad plate, you're wound way too tight. You should step out of the box more often. See what the world has to offer."

"I stepped out of the box the night I broke the statue, and look where that got me."

"Exactly! You had a chance to get to know me as a result.

Talk about lucky. Think what could happen if you tried again."

"No, thanks."

"You can't play it safe all the time."

"I don't play it safe all the time."

"Are you telling me that you weren't just calculating how much water on the floor it would take before the electrical cord for the floor polisher becomes an electrocution risk?"

I crossed my arms. He could make fun of me if he wanted. There were 550 accidental electrocution deaths in the United States last year. Most of those took place at work. Call me a fool, but water and electricity don't mix. That's why it isn't advised that you blow your hair dry in the shower. I stepped forward and grabbed the handles of the polisher. Drew raised an eyebrow, but then flipped the switch on the handle. The polisher nearly shot out of my hands. It felt like trying to hold a rodeo bull in place. I spun in a couple wide circles, trying to get it under control.

"Interesting technique," Drew yelled out over the sound of the machine.

"If *you* want to polish the floor, then you can do it your way." I turned my back on him and wrestled the machine to my will. Eventually it began to behave and glided up and down the gym parquet floor in a rough approximation of rows. I would stop every so often and squirt (a safe amount) of the combination liquid wax and cleaning gel onto the floor in front of me. I shot a few glances over at Drew, but he was busy walking up and down the bleachers, using a paint scraper to clean the bottom of each bench, then starting over at the beginning of the row to sweep the trash down to the next level.

It seemed strange not to talk, but the polisher was so loud and the gym so big that it made conversation practically impossible. It wasn't that I wanted to be insulted by Drew, the jolly janitor, but I had realized how nice it was to talk to someone about anything other than what had happened. Drew was right about one thing. As the hour went on, I felt less stiff and sore. My muscles limbered up, and when I turned the machine off, I looked back over the floor and felt a huge sense of satisfaction. I had accomplished something. It might not have been much, but it was something.

Drew was at the far end of the gym gathering all of the trash into three giant black bags. We'd finished sooner than I'd expected, and I wondered if that meant we got to knock off early or if we were expected to tackle some other chore. I had just started to make a dent in the extra credit history homework. I could use the extra time. I began to wind up the cord.

The doors to the outside burst open, and a group of guys spilled into the gym. It must have been snowing outside, because they were covered with a mix of slush and mud. One of them, a junior, gave a whoop when he saw the waxed floor. He took off at a run, dropping to his knees and sliding six or seven feet. He left a long dark smear of mud in the center of my floor.

"What the hell are you doing!" I screeched. I ran out into the middle of the floor waving my hands as if I wanted to scare off a group of wayward geese that were pooping all over my lawn.

The guys stopped in place. I looked around. They were all wearing their outdoor shoes, some with cleats and hard soles. They'd
tracked in mud, granite-colored slush, and a few random twigs.
The floor was ruined.

"Easy, Kendrick. Who made you Miss Clean?" The junior
tossed a filthy football into the net box at the end of the gym.
"We had to bring the equipment back. What's the big deal?"

"The entire floor has to be done again," I said, pointing out
the obvious.

"Isn't that what you have your townie for?" The junior
motioned to Drew, who was still standing to the side. "You keep
them around for more than just looking at, don't you? Or do
you just use them for kissing?" The other guys laughed. Drew
crossed over to us in several short strides, and the Evesham guys
suddenly bunched together.

"Is there a problem?" Drew asked. He may have been only
a few years older than the guys, but looking at them together,
it was clear it was the difference between a bunch of boys and a
man. Drew was broad through the shoulders, and his face had
clean lines, with no baby fat sticking to his cheeks. I could tell
the guys were scared that Drew would start something with
them, and I liked that. They outnumbered him eight to one, but
they were still afraid. I stood behind Drew with my arms crossed.
I hoped he would make them wipe up the slush off the floor with
their tongues.

"There's no problem, man." The junior rocked back and

forth. I think he was trying to look tough, but it looked like he was trying out for a chorus role with a production of West Side Story.

"All right, then." Drew stood his ground. The Evesham kids headed out of the gym, darting looks over their shoulders to make sure Drew wasn't following them. I pressed my lips together. I wanted to scream.

"Make sure there aren't any sloppy seconds left behind," the junior yelled, and then they all laughed, slamming the door.

I whirled on Drew. "Why didn't you make them clean that up? How can you let them get away with that?"

"You don't do a lot of meditation, do you?" Drew pulled the mop from the cart and started to wipe up the mess on the floor.

I stared at him, wondering if he'd lost his mind. "What are you talking about?"

Drew motioned to the mess on the floor. "This is just dirt. Save your wrath for something bigger than mud."

"He was rude."

"No, he was an asshole. Me telling him that isn't going to change anything. He isn't suddenly going to fall on his knees and see the light. You know what's going to happen? He's going to run to the dean and say that he was returning the ball when I forced him to clean the gym floor. His friends will back him up, and I'll be the one in trouble."

"But that isn't fair," I said, knowing I sounded like a five-year-old. "I would have backed you up."

"Nothing personal, but I'm guessing Dean Winston doesn't have your picture on the wall for Student of the Month."

My mouth snapped shut. He was right. Winston wouldn't believe me. Even if he thought I was telling the truth, he'd never admit it.

"You can go ahead and get out of here. I've got this covered," Drew said, glancing at his watch. "You put in your time."

I was tempted to take him up on his offer. I still had homework to finish. The smart thing to do would be to thank him and get the homework done. The image of my empty dorm room flashed in my mind. I didn't feel like doing the smart thing.

"It'll go faster with both of us," I said. "Besides, I've started to get the hang of this polisher."

"I noticed. I was just thinking how you were the Princess of the Polisher," Drew said, smiling.

"Master of the Mop," I said.

"Sultan of Shellac," he fired back.

I laughed, and turned my back to fire up the machine. I heard Drew call my name, and I turned around to be smacked with a blob of slush smack in the center of my chest. I stared down at the wet splotch. I looked up, and Drew's face was twitching as he tried to avoid laughing. I bent down and picked up a handful of slush.

Drew held up his hands as if he were surrendering. "I don't know what came over me."

I flung the slush ball at him and missed. "I meant to miss you. I'm showing you what a better person I am."

"Of course."

I waited until he bent over to pick up the mop handle, and then I hurled another slush ball at him, this time hitting him in the center of his butt. He turned around, wiping the rest of the slush off of his jeans. He raised an eyebrow in a silent question.

"I decided I'm not really a better person," I said.

It didn't take long to redo the floor. Turned out Drew was right, mud wipes right up. I helped put the cart back into the closet. Drew made sure everything was put back in just the right place, and he ticked off the tasks on the to-do list. He made sure the mop was clean before he hung it up to dry. He clearly took pride in his job. Once everything was properly stowed away, he grabbed his jacket off the hook.

"Here, don't forget these." I handed him the printouts of the training programs I'd found.

"Oh, right. Thanks." He pulled a book out of his coat pocket and folded the papers inside.

"What are you reading?" I asked.

Drew flipped the book over so I could see the cover. *Dante's Inferno*. I hadn't expected that. I'd seen him as more of a Stephen King fan.

"Fan of the classics, huh?" I asked, trying to hide my surprise.

"It's on the reading list. I'm trying to get a jump start."

"Reading list?"

"I'm going to Yale next year. I'm working this job to earn some extra money."

"Yale?"

"I got in last year but delayed my start. I wanted to travel a little, earn some extra cash."

I could feel my face burning. "Oh." I couldn't believe I'd given him a bunch of information on vocational programs and had acted like he would be lucky to get in. "I didn't mean to imply that the skilled trades were your only option."

"Don't worry about it. Your heart was in the right place. Besides, I thought it was kind of cool that you noticed I have good dexterity." He waved his fingers in front of my face. "I like the idea of you thinking about what my hands can do." He winked before turning to leave.

I flushed even redder. "I wasn't thinking about your hands," I called after him.

"Sure you weren't."

"I wasn't. I was trying to be nice."

Drew turned around to face me, leaning against the doorjamb. "Admit it. You're thinking about it now." He saluted and left.

I kicked the cart. Darn it. Now I *was* thinking about it.

17

The dining hall at Evesham is decorated to look like one of the halls at Oxford. The long wall has arched cathedral windows, and the ceiling is painted with vines and leaves. There are long wooden tables, and although seats aren't assigned, it's habit that the seniors sit in the back, farthest from the front faculty table. Well, at least most of them do. I'd taken to sitting by myself in the leper section near the trash cans. Out of site, out of mind. Unlike in most cafeterias, we don't wait in a line for food. Each table has menus on a clipboard, and you check off what you want and then one of the servers bring your tray.

I ticked off scrambled eggs and toast and pulled out my math homework to go over my answers one more time. My grades had gone up lately because I'd had way more time to do homework, without needing to spend time talking to anyone. Isolation has its advantages. Kelsie sat down and waved away the server. She never eats breakfast. Or to be more precise, she never eats her own breakfast. Kelsie picked the strawberry off my toast plate and popped it into her mouth.

"So how come I have to hear from someone else that you're assigned to clean with some sort of hunky man model?"

"What?"

"If I had known they hired cute townies to clean, I would have taken an interest in dust long before now." Kelsie looked around to make sure no one was paying attention to us. "Is he the one from that night?"

I rolled my eyes. "No, he is not the one."

"You're going to want to bail on breakfast, by the way."

"Why?"

"Trust me. Make yourself scarce." Kelsie took a piece of my toast and wrinkled up her nose. "I hate this whole grain stuff. The nuts get in my teeth."

"Then, get your own toast." I grabbed the piece back. "Why should I leave?"

"I can take time to explain things, or later we can talk about how next time you should listen to me," Kelsie said, pointing a pink nail in my face.

I opened my mouth to argue the point, but there was a rustle at the front of the room and Joel hopped up onto one of the tables.

"Too late," Kelsie groaned.

Joel clapped his hands to get everyone's attention. "As the

student council president I would like to call a town meeting."

I raised an eyebrow at Kelsie, who gave me a look that said I should have made a run for it when I had the chance. Town meetings are an Evesham tradition. If someone has a gripe—ranging from someone playing their music too loud (or playing music someone else can't stand) to the need for more organic veggies for the salad bar—then we are supposed to talk it out over one of our meals. It's supposed to remind us of how we would have talked over issues with our families over a dinner table. The truth is most of Evesham's students didn't have family dinners, unless you count sitting down with your nanny over fish sticks while your parents go to some fancy fund-raiser.

Joel nodded to one of the tables, and I saw Mandy Gallaway get up. She pulled her uniform skirt down and paused long enough to make sure everyone was watching her walk to the front of the room.

"Uh-oh," I said softly under my breath.

Kelsie grabbed the last piece of my toast. "File this experience under, 'Next time I will pay attention to my best friend when she gives me advice.'"

"I wanted to bring up the issue of having to be on restriction." Mandy looked around the room. "I think it's unfair that we're all on lockdown when only one person did something wrong."

There were a few grumbles from other people in the cafeteria. I stared down at my eggs so I didn't have to meet anyone's eyes. Did they think this was my idea? If Mandy wanted to go into town and flash a nipple or her thong at a random photographer, it was fine by me. If they wanted to gripe, they should take it up with Winston.

"Hailey, can you come up here and join us while we talk this out?" Joel asked.

I looked up from my eggs, my stomach flipping over. I pointed a finger at my chest, on the off chance that Joel had another Hailey in mind. He nodded, and Mandy crossed her arms over her chest with a smirk. With everyone's eyes on me, I figured bolting from the room was out. Taking a deep breath, I stood up and walked slowly to the front.

"Dean Winston imposed restriction on all of us as a way to demonstrate how we're connected. What impacts one of us impacts all of us," Joel said in his best presidential voice.

"I don't think Hailey cares how what she did impacts all of us," Mandy said. "She isn't showing Evesham school spirit. I haven't been able to go into town. I know Hailey thinks sticking up for this guy is important, but what I want to do is important too."

I fought the urge to push Mandy into a pile of pancakes. I could picture the syrup running down her face, slicking her hair down to her head.

"Of course everyone has their own unique wants and feelings, and all of those are important. Does anyone else want to share how this situation is affecting them?" Joel offered.

I turned to look at Joel. Was he kidding? I pulled on his shirt so we were closer.

"Why are you doing this?" I hissed into his ear.

"This is a reasonable way to handle the situation. People are unhappy. They want to share how they're feeling."

Joel could act as if he were doing the right thing, but I sensed that the reason he was willing to have me stand up in front of everyone and be humiliated had to due with him being upset by what I'd said to Tristan on Saturday night.

"You can't do this," I whispered to him.

"Mandy went to Winston. This is his idea," Joel whispered back. He shrugged slightly. My lips pressed together. Joel was going to stand there and play the party line. What Winston wanted, he would do.

A freshman in the front row raised her hand. "I think it's disgusting that you cheated on your boyfriend," she said. She shot a look at Mandy, who nodded her approval. I had the feeling the room was stacked with people that Mandy had spoon-fed comments to. We'd be there all morning hearing what a lousy person I was.

"I have to go to the bathroom," I said.

"You can't leave," Mandy said. "You have to stand here while everyone gets their say."

"Fine, but do you mind if I go to the bathroom first? There isn't a rule against that, is there?"

"It's important that you understand how what you've done affects everyone," Joel said.

I clenched my teeth. "I'll be right back."

I stepped into the hallway and crossed to the ladies' room. I shut the door behind me and leaned against it. I didn't plan to stand in front of the whole school while everyone listed out how I was making their lives miserable because they couldn't get to the mall.

I cracked the door open and peeped out. Mandy was standing in the doorway to the cafeteria, watching the hall. There was no way I was going to be able to sneak past her and out of the building. I wondered how long I could stay in the bathroom before they sent someone in after me. I looked at my watch. There was another thirty minutes left until the first bell. Way too long. I felt my stomach turn over again. I felt like I might throw up my eggs. Maybe if I vomited, people would consider it sufficient apology, but I doubted it. They were going to make me stand there and just take it.

A car horn outside honked, and it made me look up. Above the stalls there was a long thin frosted window. I stepped up onto one of the toilets and slid the window open. The window faced the alley behind the cafeteria building. There was a Dumpster directly below. It was insane. Most likely I wouldn't even fit, the window was so narrow. Besides, I would only be putting off the inevitable. Sooner or later I would have to face the music.

My heart was pounding. All I wanted to do was escape. I heard Mandy's high shrill laugh from the hall. That decided it.

I pulled myself up onto the ledge and swung one foot out the window, and then the other. I started to lower myself down. My uniform skirt was caught in the window, and I could feel it hitching up. Great. Now my bare butt was on the outside of the window while the rest of me was still inside the bathroom. My feet swung around, feeling for the edges of the Dumpster, but all I felt was empty space. I tried to lower myself farther, but the combination of my skirt and blazer bunched up was keeping me from sliding down any more. This wasn't going to work.

I tried to pull myself back up through the window. My arms were shaking from the effort, but I wasn't moving. Great. I was stuck in the window. What's worse than being called to the front of your entire school and humiliated? Being caught trying to sneak away with your skirt up over your waist and your panty-clad butt hanging out over the cafeteria Dumpster.

"Well, here's something you don't see every day," a voice said in the alley.

My head shot straight up. I knew that voice. "Drew?"

"Hailey?" He sounded shocked. "Looks like you need some help."

"I don't *need* help, but some help would be appreciated."

"Looks to me like you need help. Do you know you're wearing Thursday panties and today's Monday?"

I blushed. "My grandma buys these for me. Stop looking at my butt," I demanded.

"It's sort of a focal point from out here."

"Help me out of here." I wiggled my legs. "Hurry up. I'm in sort of a situation."

I could hear him climbing up onto the Dumpster behind me. "You know, there's a waitlist to get into this place. You don't see many trying to get out. At least this way." His hand was on my leg. "I'm going to heft you up a bit and then pull you out."

"Watch your hands," I warned him.

"I am watching them."

I could hear voices from the hallway. It was just a matter of time before Mandy busted her way in, and then there would be no amount of explaining that would make things right.

Drew held me around the waist, and I felt myself start to slide backward. I held on to the window ledge.

"Rest your feet on the rim of the Dumpster."

I slid until my feet were resting next to Drew's feet and my face was still looking through the window. I used one hand to jam my skirt back down into place.

"Okay. Hang on to the window while I get down, and then I'll help you."

Through the window I could see the bathroom door start to open. I threw myself into Drew, and we dropped to the ground in a heap. I landed on top of him, and he gave a loud "Ooph."

I held my finger over my mouth, indicating he needed to be quiet.

"She's not in here." Mandy's voice drifted down from the window.

Drew raised an eyebrow. He stood and pulled me up. His shirt was smeared with ketchup. He jerked his head to the right, indicating that I should follow him, and I did. His truck was parked at the end of the alley.

When we reached it, he turned back to me. "You need a ride somewhere?" He held up a hand. "I mean, of course, that you don't *need* a ride, but would one be helpful?"

I wiped my hand across my face. I was shaking. I didn't know what to do. I couldn't go back inside.

"I can't leave campus."

"No, you're not *supposed* to leave. But I'm betting you're capable. Rules are meant to be broken."

"I've never skipped school in my life," I protested.

Drew's eyes went wide like a kid who had just spotted Santa Claus. "Really? Your first time? Oh, that's exciting." He rubbed his hands together. "This will be good. Time's wasting. Let's go." He motioned to his truck.

I held back. "I'll get in trouble."

"News flash, Prima Donna. You're already in trouble. There's no death penalty for skipping school. If you're already in trouble, why not go really big? Are you telling me you had the guts to sneak out of a place by jumping into a Dumpster, but then you were just going to go right back inside? Besides, with what they charge for tuition for this place, they aren't going to kick you out for skipping one day. It wouldn't be cost efficient."

My mind raced. I hadn't thought through this plan very well. Everything had been based on the idea of getting away. I heard a burst of laughter, and at the other end of the alley I could see a few Evesham students making their way over to a classroom building. At the very least I needed more time to think of what to do. "I'll go with you," I said.

"Allow me," he said, bowing low and opening the door.

18

I wasn't sure what I'd expected. I'd never snuck off campus before. I guess I thought Drew might race the truck toward the gates while the security team released savage German shepherds and shot up the back window in a blaze of gunfire. Drew had me sit on the passenger-side floor, and he tossed his coat over the top of my head. He eased up to the security gate at the front of campus and casually chatted with the guard—someone named Earl—for a few minutes about football, before we pulled away. There were no alarms, no searchlights, no police barricades. The whole thing was almost anticlimactic.

"You can sit up now," Drew said.

I pulled myself up and clicked the seat belt. The vinyl seats of the truck were patched here and there with duct tape. The truck was old. It had a tape deck. My legs were bare and covered with goose bumps. I pulled my socks up to cover as much real estate as possible.

Drew slammed his hand against the dashboard. "Sorry. The heater is kind of dodgy." He slammed his hand again, and then a rush of hot air whooshed out of the vent. "Are you freezing? There's a sweatshirt in the back somewhere."

Without looking he hooked his arm over the back of the seat and started fishing around in the pile of junk that was in the back of the cab. There seemed to be an array of books, sporting gear, and clothing. Like a magician with a rabbit, he yanked a sweatshirt out of the middle of the pile. There was a Boston Bruins logo across the front. He handed it to me. I held it pinched between two fingers.

"It's clean," Drew said, looking over at me with a smile. "At least, there's no Ebola on it or anything."

"Of course. I wasn't thinking that." I gave it a quick sniff test. It didn't smell funny. In fact it smelled nice, like pine trees. I pulled it on over my sweater. I pulled the length of it over my knees. "Where are we going?"

"Your first skip day." Drew shook his head as if he were overcome by the enormity of it all. "We have to do something good. You can't waste something like that. We'll get some breakfast at Denny's and come up with a plan."

"Who's Denny?"

Drew laughed. "You're joking, right? Denny's? As in Denny's restaurant?"

"Oh, right. Of course."

Drew stopped the truck in the middle of the road. "You've never been to a Denny's, have you?"

"I have been to a Denny's. My family stopped at one once when we were driving to New York."

"You didn't eat there, did you? You went there for the bathroom."

"Don't make a federal case out of it." I pulled my hands up into the sleeves of the sweatshirt.

"Where does your family go for breakfast?"

"Will you just drive? God. We go out. We just don't go to Denny's. There are other places to eat, you know."

Drew put the truck back into drive, and we headed toward town. "Where do you go? Four Seasons?"

"You have some sort of obsession for Denny's, don't you? Were you raised by wolves in a Denny's parking lot?" I shifted in the seat. I wasn't going to tell him, but we did used to go to the Four Seasons for Sunday brunch. My mom used to love their smoked salmon eggs Benedict.

"Your first Grand Slam *and* your first skip day. I feel like we should get a picture taken or something. You could frame it later for your fireplace mantel. A person never forgets their first Slam."

I had no idea what he was talking about. I'd thought a grand slam had something to do with baseball. Was he planning to take me to a game? Did anyone even play baseball this time of year?

We pulled into the Denny's parking lot, and I followed Drew inside. The restaurant seemed to be decorated in orange and yellow surfaces that all could be cleaned with a power washer—vinyl seats, tile floors, laminate countertops. Given the amount of grease that seemed to be in the air, it probably took a pressure washer to get this place clean. Drew walked right past the WAIT HERE TO BE SEATED sign and grabbed a couple of menus out of the server's lectern, waving at the cook as he walked by. The cook waved back with a spatula. Why was I not surprised he was a regular?

"Hey, darling! I'll bring you some coffee," a waitress called out. Drew slid into a booth and motioned for me to take the other seat. He began to pore over the menu as if it contained the secret of the universe. I sat down and touched the tabletop carefully, looking for any random sticky spots. There were a few places where cigarette butts had burned the laminate, back in the days when smoking in restaurants was legal. The waitress came by, dropping two coffee cups out from under her arm and artfully pouring coffee into them before they had even stopped rattling on the tabletop. Her other hand held a rag that looked like it had last been clean around the turn of the century, and she used it to wipe the table down, no doubt smearing bacteria all over. Drew could mock the Four Seasons if he liked, but there was something to be said for fresh linen tablecloths.

The waitress looked me over, noting my uniform skirt. She raised an eyebrow at Drew. I was impressed she could lift it, given the amount of foundation that was on her face.

"We're going to need a range of things here. I'm not sure we can choose. We'll have the All-American Slam, a Lumberjack Slam, a side of biscuits and sausage gravy, the smothered hash browns . . . oh, and some pancakes. Are you still doing that stuffed French toast, too? The one with the strawberries?" Drew ran his finger down the menu to make sure there wasn't anything he had forgotten.

"You got it, Drew. You need cream for the coffee, sweetheart?"

I looked down at the coffee. "Do you make lattes?"

"Does this look like Starbucks?" She asked with a snap of her gum.

"Right. I'll have the cream." I considered asking her if they could warm the cream up in the back, but I decided it wouldn't go over well, and with my luck she would spit in my eggs. Drew gave a nod to the busboy as he passed with his tub of dirty dishes.

"Do you know every Denny's employee, or just the ones that work at this location?" I asked him.

"I used to work here in the kitchen, and I still help out once in a while if they're short staffed."

"Can't resist the allure of the food, huh?"

"Can't resist the extra cash. Somehow I managed to misplace my trust fund, so I've got to stockpile as much as I can for Yale."

I wasn't sure exactly how much Yale cost, but I knew it wasn't cheap. I was worried enough about getting in. I couldn't imagine worrying about how to pay for it too.

"Maybe you can get a scholarship," I suggested. "There's all kinds of information about that stuff online."

Drew cocked his head and looked at me. "Careful, or I'm going to start thinking you care. Don't you worry about me. I've applied for loans and grants, and that fancy school of yours pays pretty good to clean desks. I'll come up with the money." He rubbed his hands together. "Now we have to decide what to do with the day."

"Why do we have to do anything?"

"Because this is found time. It's a gift. Where should you be right now?"

I looked over at the yellowing plastic clock that hung on the wall. "Math."

"Now, isn't this better than math?" Drew motioned around the room.

"I'm withholding judgment at this point."

"Now you're just being a snot. If you're going to skip, then you have to do something worthwhile. Otherwise the trouble won't be worth it." Drew snapped his fingers. "We could go skiing."

I looked at him. Was he nuts? "I don't know how to ski."

"You look like you have the capacity to learn. I can spot talent. You look like a natural. Didn't your mom and dad ever take you to Aspen? Maybe doing a bit of snow time with the royal family in the Alps?"

"No." I sipped the coffee. It wasn't bad. "I can't say the queen and I have done a lot of snowboarding."

The waitress was back. She filled the table with plates. "The French toast is still coming."

I poked the gray object on the plate in front of me with my fork. It looked like it might fight back.

"Biscuits with sausage gravy. Looks disgusting, tastes great." Drew jabbed his fork in and held a clump of it out in front of my face. He waved it back and forth in front of my lips. "Open up, or I'm going to start making choo-choo noises."

I opened my mouth, and he popped the food in. I was prepared for it to taste like dryer lint covered in Elmer's glue, but it was actually sort of tasty.

"Ah, not bad, huh?" Drew stuck the fork back in and ate some. "Try the hash browns. Give that Four Seasons palate a good grease wash."

I wasn't crazy about the hash browns—they were too greasy for me—but the French toast when it arrived was beyond divine. Drew clearly took his eating seriously, because he didn't attempt conversation while we ate. He would look up and smile every so often, but otherwise he was focused on his food.

I wondered what was going to happen when I went back to school. The top of Winston's head was going to lift off when he found out what I'd done. Drew was right that there was no death penalty, but Dean Winston was going to come up with something. Something that might make me wish for death. Winston struck me as the kind of guy terrorists call when they're looking for new ideas. I stared out the window. He might expel me, despite what Drew said about the school wanting the tuition money. My grandma would freak out if I got kicked out of school. No one in our family had ever been expelled. And I was pretty sure an expulsion would blow my chances with Yale. It wasn't the kind of school that catered to the juvenile delinquent crowd. I wouldn't be surprised if Winston was already contacting the admissions office, telling them that I was the type to spray paint my name on Yale's Harkness Tower, or beat up the mascot bulldog.

Drew leaned back from the table. "All right. Now tell me everything."

"Why?"

"Because I'm interested, and you want to talk about it."

"No, I don't."

"Liar. You think I won't know how to help you, but that's where you're wrong." He raised his hand to cut me off before I could say anything. "Admit it. You were wrong about me before. I happen to be a keen problem solver. Sometime I'll tell you about the time I had my wallet lifted in the Cairo market, and I followed the guy and won it back in a game of dice, along with an extra hundred bucks."

"You traveled through Egypt?" I had pictured Drew as the kind of guy who didn't travel out of the state, let alone the country. Maybe down South to some kind of barbecue championship event, but exotic travel had never occurred to me. "Did you see the pyramids?"

"That's what you pay attention to? I tell you I managed to infiltrate a den of thieves and win, and you focus on the pyramids? If you don't mind me being so blunt, that's part of your problem. You focus on the wrong things." He leaned back into the corner of the booth so that his crossed feet hung out into the aisle. "Telling someone who has no connection to a situation gives you a fresh view. You could use a fresh pair of eyes. Now, start at the beginning. You decided to attack the school mascot because . . ."

I looked into his eyes. I *could* use a new perspective. It wasn't like I had any great ideas on my own.

"I'm going to need more coffee," I said. "It's a long story."

Drew raised his finger, and the waitress headed in our direction. I took a deep breath and tried to figure out where to start.

19

When I stopped speaking, Drew leaned back and said nothing. I sipped my coffee to have something to do. I was practically humming with all the caffeine in my system. If anyone looked directly at me, I bet I would be a blur.

"So, as you can see, it's pretty screwed up," I said, wanting him to say something.

"You did a good thing."

"Are you kidding? I haven't done anything right since this whole thing started. It was like I took one wrong turn and now I can't get my life back on track."

"I don't know. Seems like you've done some good things. You took the heat so your friend Joel doesn't lose his scholarship. That shows character. Sad truth is that most people only do the right thing if it doesn't cost them anything."

I shrugged off his praise. "How much character does it show

that I kissed my boyfriend's best friend?" I left off the part that really scared me. Not only had I kissed him, but I'd liked it.

"Well, I'll divide my answer to that question into two parts. How much character is Tristan showing? He won't even give you a chance to explain."

"You don't understand. Tristan has issues around trust."

"We all have issues. If you want to worry about issues, worry less about his and focus on why you kissed this Joel guy in the first place."

"I told you. It was a heat-of-the-moment thing."

"Uh-huh." Drew smirked and looked out the window.

"It was," I said.

"If that's what you want to think, that's fine with me."

I crossed my arms and tapped my foot on the floor. "So you think it's something else. You have some explanation for the whole thing. Go on, share your wisdom."

Drew turned around so that his feet were on the floor and he was staring me straight in the eyes. "You kissed Joel as a way to break up with Tristan."

I laughed and looked away. "Are you kidding me? Why would I want to break up with him? Tristan's the perfect boyfriend. We've been together for years."

"You're not in love with him."

"And you know how I feel better than I do? That's amazing." I couldn't believe him. His brain must have been clogged with the amount of grease he'd consumed. He had bacon brain. "You must be some kind of psychic, since you know things about me that even I don't know."

"Tell me why you love him," Drew said.

"You want a list, fine. He's nice. I can depend on him. He's very loyal." I started ticking off items on my fingers.

"You make him sound like a cocker spaniel. That's not love. That's affection. He's a habit. Deep down you want to break the habit, so you did the one thing you knew he wouldn't be able to stand. You kissed someone else, and now you're free. You're scared to be off track, but I think you're sick of always living in the lines. Maybe you wanted to explore what you might find if you wandered away from the tracks just a bit. Best part of being lost, you know, is discovering things you didn't know you were looking for."

Just my luck. In addition to his keen cleaning abilities and skill at rolling dice with Egyptian thieves, he was also a philosopher. "That's absurd. I'm not sick of living 'in the lines' of my life. My life was going just fine before all of this."

"Really? What about the situation with your dad?"

"A person can be disappointed in something without it meaning they want their entire life to be different."

"Why didn't you tell your dad that it wasn't okay for him to ruin your summer by bailing on you?"

"It's not that simple. He has to go. It's his job."

"Ah, slave labor program." He laughed at my expression. "Don't get yourself all riled up. All I'm saying is that people act like they're stuck, when the truth is that they have a choice. Your dad doesn't have to do that job, and you don't have to be the good girl all the time. You don't have to keep dating Tristan just because you did for years. If you want to be happy, then you have to make it happen."

"Well, this has been very helpful," I said, rolling my eyes. "Your words of wisdom will make all the trouble I'm going to get in for skipping worthwhile."

Drew stood up, smiling. He was either ignoring my sarcasm or had missed it completely. "You're welcome, but you're going to get even more bang for your buck. I thought of something we can do."

"I should go back."

"You're already in trouble. Might as well make it count. Besides, you're going to love this." Drew left some money on the table for the waitress and started walking out. He stopped at the counter and said something to the cook. The cook passed him two giant metal trays. They looked like cookie sheets on steroids.

"What are those for?"

"Wait and see."

"Where are we going?" I trailed after him. I felt nervous; God only knew what he had planned.

Drew stopped to hold the door open. "Prima Donna, you cannot even imagine how much fun you're going to have. But first I'm going to introduce you to another place I'm willing to bet you've never been to." He paused for dramatic effect. "We're going to Walmart. You're going to love it. It's like a redneck version of Harrods."

20

Five hours later I sat outside Dean Winston's office trying to ignore the glances his secretary kept shooting in my direction. I couldn't tell if it was because she knew how much trouble I was in, or because of my outfit.

Drew had made all my fashion choices at Walmart. He'd decreed that my school uniform was not appropriate for the activity he had planned. I ended up wearing black and yellow striped tights that were a leftover from a Halloween costume that didn't sell. Over those I wore a pair of black snow pants decorated with fake spray painted tags. Across my bum in purple letters with silver trim was the word "RADICAL." There was a "Kilroy Was Here" on one knee, and running down the side was a bright yellow cursive "Anarchy." I was still wearing my uniform blouse with Drew's Bruins sweatshirt over the top. My new red gloves were normal, but after Drew declared my head to be freakishly small, I ended up with a hat from the kid's department, complete with earflaps and a pom-pom on top. It was decorated with various glittery fairy decals. I reached a hand up to touch it. It was the tackiest thing I had ever seen, and I loved it.

My face was windburned. We'd gone sledding. I hadn't been sledding since I was a little kid, and I couldn't remember when I'd had so much fun. I wasn't as fearless as Drew. He liked to get a running start and then fling himself facedown onto the giant metal tray, barreling down the hill. I preferred to sit at the top on the tray and then inch myself forward until gravity kicked in and carried me to the bottom, but I loved the rush of the wind. The air was so cold that it seemed hot and burning when I sucked it in. It felt like it was scouring my lungs clean. As soon as I came to a stop at the bottom, I would pop up and do my best to run up the hill so I could go again. For the first time since this whole mess had started, my mind had stopped spinning around with everything that had happened. I didn't think about my dad, Tristan, Joel, or anyone else at Evesham. I didn't even worry about sledding injury rates. We went sledding until my legs were rubbery from walking up the hill in the deep snow, and the sweatshirt was damp from melted snow and sweat.

As Drew drove me back to the school, he gave me advice on how to handle Winston. "Tell him you felt mentally unstable. That you were so emotionally damaged that you were afraid you might 'do something' so you ran away to clear your head. Trust me. The last thing this guy wants on his hands is a suicidal student. Boarding schools live in fear of that stuff. It's bad for public relations."

"You should let me out here," I said, motioning for Drew to pull over a block or so before the school gates.

"What? Is this one of those things where you're embarrassed to be seen with me?" Drew made a face as if he were deeply wounded.

I smacked him on his shoulder. "I get sarcasm for trying to keep you out of trouble? I save your job, your financial ticket to Yale, and you mock me? This will be the last time I'll take all the heat."

Drew laughed. "I would be happy to be the Clyde in your Bonnie and Clyde lawless adventure."

Bonnie and Clyde were lovers. I wondered if that was why Drew had used that example. As soon as the thought flashed through my mind, I felt myself flush. Apparently, since the Joel incident I was incapable of having interactions with a guy without wondering if he liked me.

"I should get going," I said, cracking the door open. "Thanks for making my first skip day so memorable."

"It's all memorable with me," Drew said with a wink before driving off.

I went directly to Dean Winston's office and told him that my delicate emotional state had snapped in the dining hall. I'd had to walk away before I did something . . . desperate. I made sure my voice had a slight quaver in it. Drew had warned me not to argue but to admit I was in the wrong. Winston glowered at me across his desk. I could see him thinking through his options. I could tell he wanted to yell, but he was uncertain. He made me wait outside his office while he decided what to do. There was a puddle of slush on the floor by my feet. I'd been at Evesham for four years, and I'd spent more time in Winston's office in the past couple weeks than I had in the entire rest of the time I'd attended the school.

Dean Winston opened the door and motioned me inside. I stood, saying a quick mental prayer that Drew was right and I wasn't about to hear that I was expelled. Drew had kept pointing out that expelled kids don't pay tuition and Winston would be crazy to kick me out over one day of skipping. People like Dean Winston would think through the economics of the situation before doing anything rash.

"The deterioration of your behavior is very troubling to me, Ms. Kendrick."

I looked down at my shoes and watched a rivulet of slush start to wind its way to the thick rug in the middle of the room. He took a step closer and put his arm around my shoulder. I felt myself tense up, and I had to fight the urge to pull away.

"I hope you know you can talk with me if you're going through a difficult time. I know these years as girls grow into young women are challenging."

I stayed perfectly still. Winston sounded like one of those films they showed us in junior high about menstruation and how we shouldn't be scared if hair started to grow on our bodies in new places. I made a noncommittal sound.

"I want you to be honest with me. Did you sneak into town to see the boy? The one you were with the night of the incident with the statue?"

"What? No." I met his stare. "I promise you I was not with the guy from that night."

Winston sat down and guided me into the chair next to him. "It isn't uncommon for young girls to become"—he searched for the right word—"enamored of the 'bad boy.' Maybe it feels daring or exciting, but you need to be careful."

Oh, god. Dean Winston was going to start talking about safe sex. "I'm not dating anyone from town," I said, hoping to cut him off. "I'm not dating anyone now."

"You're a very fortunate young lady, and part of that fortune is that you're being protected from some of the unseemly sides of life. There are people who would want to take advantage of you, to use any relationship for their own gains. Nothing against anyone from town, but they would certainly be aware that you come from a prestigious family."

"So you think anyone from town would only be seeing me for my money?"

Winston patted me on the knee. "Of course not." He waited a beat before continuing. "But this can't be something you're sure about. People aren't always open about their motivations. In general I think you'll find it's best when people stick with their own kind. Not that I'm advocating that anyone is better than anyone else, but you come from different worlds."

"Different worlds," I repeated. "Got it."

"Normally anyone who skips class is placed on restriction. Now, you're already on restriction, so that isn't really an option for us."

"I understand." I really hoped Winston wasn't going to do the thing where he asked me what I felt a reasonable punishment would be.

"If you'll tell me who else was involved in the earlier incident, then I'm prepared to consider things wrapped up and behind us."

"I can't."

Mr. Winston sighed as if I had caused him a deep grievous harm. "There's a difference between 'can't' and 'won't,' Ms. Kendrick. Very well. We're going to continue with your existing punishment. The restriction stands for you and your classmates. You're going to write a letter of apology to each of your instructors for missing today's classes and prepare for me a written report on the history of the school. Also, I'm going to require that you meet with the school counselor."

I nodded. I figured I was going to have to see Ms. Sullivan once I brought up the whole emotional fragility thing. I had zero interest in spending time spilling my guts to the school counselor, but I didn't see any way out of it.

"All right. I've already called Ms. Sullivan, and she's cleared her schedule to see you."

He stood, and I let out a deep breath. I wasn't going to be expelled. There was a tap at the door, and Kelsie stood there.

"I brought over Hailey's things that she left in the dining hall." Kelsie held out my books.

"Very well. Don't dawdle, Ms. Kendrick. Ms. Sullivan will be waiting for you in her office."

I nodded and followed Kelsie out into the hall. Our footsteps echoed on the wooden floors. We walked past the framed photos of various Evesham graduation classes. I felt the eyes of all the past students watching us go by. Ms. Sullivan's office was down a level on the first floor, in a room she'd decorated to look like someone's grandmother's overly fussy formal living room. Kelsie waited to say anything until we hit the stairwell. She shot a look over her shoulder to make sure Mr. Winston wasn't following us.

"Where the hell did you go?"

"You told me to leave. I was just taking your advice."

"Did you seriously crawl out the bathroom window?" Kelsie giggled. "You should have seen Mandy when she figured out you were gone. She was practically foaming at the mouth. No one could figure out where you went. That one freshman girl who is always doing tarot cards actually wondered out loud if you'd disappeared. She thinks maybe the guy from town is a ghost or a vampire or something and that's why you can't tell anyone who he is."

"She's got to lay off watching all those paranormal TV shows."

"She's hoping you're dating the undead, because it gives her

hope that all her *Twilight* dreams might actually come true."
Kelsie stopped me on the landing. "Okay, be honest now. Why
are you dressed like you're homeless?"

"You don't like the hat?" I fluffed my pom-pom.

"I would burn it before I would let it touch my head."

"Well, don't come begging me to borrow it later when it
catches on as a trend."

"Where did you go?"

"I went sledding."

"Sledding?"

"And to Denny's." I broke into a smile. "I had a Grand Slam."

"I have no idea what's going on with you," Kelsie said.

"I know. I don't know what's going on with me either, but
I'm not sure it's all bad." I hugged her, took my books, and loped
down the rest of the stairs to meet with Ms. Sullivan.

21

My favorite building on campus is the library. I love the smell of books and how the silence makes the place feel special, almost sacred. The corner of the library is a three-story stone turret room with thin windows. The room is full of several long wooden tables set with green banker lights making puddles of yellow light. Each of the windows is set out slightly, creating a small window seat. I always grab one of those to work in. It isn't as easy as having the table as a desk, but I like to lean against the cool stone and look out the leaded glass windows. It feels like being inside a castle. A castle where you would never run out of things to read. Most of the students at Evesham don't use the library often; they prefer to do their research online. As far as I'm concerned, the fact that it is often empty makes it even better.

My meeting with Ms. Sullivan had gone okay. I think she was excited to have a potential crisis on her hands. Her job had to be pretty boring most of the time, with people only showing up to talk about college admission options, roommate conflicts, and the occasional bout of homesickness. It would be like being a doctor where people only came into the office to have splinters removed or with stuffed-up noses. You'd have to look forward to someone coming in with a lawn mower amputation of the foot or a good cardiac condition. Most likely, thinking I was on the verge of an emotional breakdown had made her entire week. She got almost giddy when she saw a long scratch on my arm that I'd gotten while sledding. Ms. Sullivan thought she might have a cutter on her hands, and I could practically see her lift out of her seat in excitement. I'd hoped I would get away with just the one meeting, but apparently she didn't think my emotionally fragile state could be repaired that quickly. I was going to have to see her weekly until she decided I was stable. I was tempted to make up multiple personalities to keep things lively for her, but I figured if I wasn't careful I'd end up in the psychiatric wing of the hospital.

The librarian had helped me pull information on the history of Evesham. I carried the dusty pile of materials back to my window seat. I'd brought my cashmere wrap with me, and my plan was to curl up and pound out the paper for Winston. I propped my feet up on the bench, tucking my wrap in around my legs. I pulled the first book off the stack and opened it up. It was dark outside, so the windows mirrored back the inside of the room. My eyes caught a reflection, and I saw that there was someone sitting off to the side watching me. Great. Ever since Drew had dropped me back at school, I'd felt like a creature at the zoo. Every time I walked into a room, everyone stopped talking and stared. The story of my great escape had spread all over campus. I couldn't tell if they were impressed with what I had done or were waiting for me to do something else unexpected at any moment.

I shifted in the seat, turning my shoulder to my new stalker, and tried to focus on the book. I read a few lines, but my eyes kept darting back to the reflection to see if the person was still watching. Finally I turned around so I could see who it was and hopefully embarrass them into moving along.

My eyes went wide. It was Tristan. He sat at one of the long tables, just staring at me. He didn't have any books with him; he wasn't even pretending to do anything else. The book I'd been holding slipped out of my hands and smacked loudly onto the marble floor, making me flinch. Tristan stood and shuffled over. I pulled my knees up so there was room, and he sat across from me in the window seat, our feet lined up in the middle and our knees making two mountains to separate us.

"You okay?" Tristan asked, his voice low and quiet even though we were the only ones in the library.

I nodded. "You okay?" My heart was beating fast. We were having an actual conversation. No ignoring each other, no screaming, just talking.

He shrugged and looked out the window, his reflection staring right back at him. "Some people are saying you snapped this morning and Dean Winston found you wandering around and brought you back."

"Not exactly. I couldn't handle the dining hall meeting thing, so I bolted. I went into town for a while to think. I came back on my own."

"You skipped classes?"

"Can you believe it?" I asked, trying to make him laugh, or at least smile. Tristan used to tease me about being a rule follower. He would say there was never a guideline I didn't embrace.

"These days there are a lot of things about you that I can't believe," he said, looking at his lap.

So much for trying to lighten the mood. "I'm sorry. I really, really am."

"What do you want to happen now?" Tristan picked at the hem on his sweater, pulling a thread loose. "Do you want to be with this guy?"

"No." My heart sped up, and I was glad I wasn't hooked to a lie detector test. I didn't want to date Joel. I was almost sure of it, but I couldn't deny there had been something that night, and that meant I was attracted either to Joel or to the idea of kissing someone else.

"Do you want us to get back together?"

My heart skipped a beat. I couldn't tell if he was asking me out of curiosity or if he thought he might be able to forgive me. Suddenly I had an image of Drew sitting at Denny's telling me that what I really wanted was to break up with Tristan. I shook my head slightly to clear his voice out of my mind. Getting back together with Tristan would be a huge step forward to getting my life back.

"I never wanted us to be apart," I said softly. I touched his wrist. He didn't pull away, so I left my finger resting there. I could feel his pulse just below the skin. "I want to be able to explain, to give you a good reason for everything that's happened, but I don't have a good reason. I screwed up." A tear ran down my face, and I wiped it away quickly. I didn't want him to think I was relying on guilt.

"You want me to say it's okay, that I forgive you, but it's not that easy. I always felt I could trust you, and then this happened. Everything feels upside down."

"I know."

"What do we do now?" Tristan asked.

I felt a brief flash of annoyance. Why did I always have to be the one to make decisions? What was I supposed to say? Was the choice over whether we got back together really in my hands? I always picked the movies and where we went to eat. Wasn't this one of the decisions Tristan should make on his own?

"What do you want to happen?" I asked.

Tristan didn't answer. I couldn't tell if that was because he didn't want to tell me, or if he didn't know himself. Maybe he was trying to keep me on my toes.

"Are you and your dad still fighting?" Tristan asked, changing the subject. He saw the confusion on my face. "Kelsie told me everything, about him bailing on your summer plans."

"I was counting on him, on our plans. Then, with everything that's happened, he's not exactly pleased with me these days. I feel like he and I need to hash things out."

"What good does that do? Do you think he'll change his mind?"

I slumped against the wall. "No." My dad and I still hadn't talked since the call with Dean Winston. He'd sent me an e-mail that he was out of town for a business trip and that he was still trying to determine what punishment he wanted to add over the whole statue incident. I hadn't bothered to write back. What would I say? He'd perfected the fine art of ignoring me the past few years. It only seemed fair that I do the best I could to try ignoring him for a change.

"Not having the end-of-summer party won't be that big a deal."

"Mandy practically considers it the crime of the century. You would think I'd canceled her birthday." I sighed. "It's not really the party that matters."

"I know. It's your dad's loss, not having the summer with you. You can't get time back."

"Thanks."

"I keep thinking that we won't be able to make up time either. We already didn't have much time left," Tristan said. "Just the rest of this year, and then you're gone for the summer, and then college for you after that."

I didn't say anything. Tristan and I had never talked about what would happen after senior year. I knew he wasn't happy that I was going away for college, but he also knew it wasn't reasonable to ask me to not apply to the schools I really wanted to go to. I knew there were millions of high school couples facing the same issue, but it was different for us. We'd spent almost every day of our lives together for the past four years. We were like a married couple that just happened to live in different dorm rooms. Our parents weren't around to tell us to take things easy. We spent more time with each other than with our families. It had a way of making things more intense. We'd dealt with the end of school by ignoring it altogether. Maybe Drew was right. Maybe I had wanted to bring things to a definite end rather than let them slowly die out in a painful long-distance relationship.

Tristan stood. "I want things to go back, but I honestly don't know if they can. That's what I came to tell you. I hate that we're not talking. A million times a day I go to tell you something, that my dad got the part in the movie he wanted, or that I heard there are those brownies you like on the menu for dinner, or to ask you what you think I should do for my senior thesis project in government, and then I remember all over again what happened."

"I don't think we can go back," I said. Tristan looked down at me. "We either go forward or we don't, but there is no going back. I'd understand if you didn't want to, but if you do, I'm here."

22

I sat straight up in bed. I looked at my clock and saw it was six a.m. I couldn't figure out what had woken me up. After Tristan had left the library, at first I didn't think I'd be able to focus. I wondered if there was something else that I should have said. There was no telling if I was going to get a chance to talk with him like that again. I could have thrown myself into his arms or begged for him to take me back. I suspected that was what he'd expected me to do. Then in the middle of worrying, my mind cleared out and I was able to bury myself in the history of Evesham. I stayed at the library until it closed just before eleven, and brought a few of the books back with me to my room. I'd actually found myself caught up in the project and hadn't turned my light out until after one a.m. I was exhausted, and now, for some reason, I was awake.

I closed my eyes and lay back down. I pulled my pink comforter up over my shoulders. I didn't have to get up for another hour. I could push it to an hour and half if I was willing to skip breakfast. After my Denny's gorging session yesterday, I wasn't sure I'd be able to face breakfast for a long time anyway. Then I heard it, a scratching sound. I pushed the covers off and crawled out of bed. I walked over to my door and leaned against it, pressing my ear to the wood. Then the sound happened again.

I unlocked the door and cracked it open to see what was causing the noise. Kelsie slid inside, looking behind her to make sure no one had seen her. Suddenly my best friend was James Bond.

I stood there in an old pair of Tristan's boxers and a T-shirt I'd bought on vacation to New York a few years ago. I rubbed the sleep out of my eyes. Kelsie wasn't normally an early bird. In fact, I couldn't remember the last time I had seen her up at this hour. Last year we had a fire drill for the dorms first thing in the morning, and Kelsie refused to get up for it. When Ms. Estes tried to get her in trouble for not evacuating, Kelsie did research to prove there was such as a thing as a "right to burn."

"What's up?" I asked.

Kelsie pulled a stack of magazines out from under her arm. "I bribed one of the maids to pick these up last night at the 7-Eleven. It hit the Web on TMZ."

"What are you talking about?"

Kelsie thrust the magazines in front of me. On top was *In Touch*, the cover story something to do with a reality star who had been caught with someone else's husband. I looked down at it and then over at Kelsie. I was a fan of reality TV as much as the next person, but it didn't strike me as the kind of thing that was worth waking up at dawn for. I searched my mind to see if the star was someone related to anyone at Evesham. Kelsie grabbed the magazine out of my hand, flipped through it, and handed it back to me.

Spoiled Heiress Breaks Hollywood Hearts—Boarding School Girl Goes Wild! There was a large photo of Tristan, posing in between his parents outside of some premier, then an inset photo of him turning away from the camera. I couldn't tell when or where the photo had been taken, but it was framed to make it look like Tristan was upset. Knowing Tristan, he could have been joking around, or hungry, or ticked about the Yankees losing, but the photo was captioned: "The brokenhearted heartthrob." My heart stopped. At the bottom of the page was a grainy photo of me. It was a picture taken at Evesham. I was walking on campus, and my mouth was open in a way that looked like I was sneering. There was also a small inset picture, my photo from last year's yearbook.

I felt the blood drain out of my face. I sat down quickly on the bed. "Are you kidding me?" I flipped through the pages. I couldn't focus on the words. They seemed to shimmy and dance across the page. Tristan had been in the tabloid magazines dozens of times because of his parents, but this was my first time. Unless you count a picture that was in *People* a couple years ago, where I was blending into the background at a party at his parents' house. Someone more famous had their elbow in front of my face in the shot. You wouldn't even have known it was me unless someone told you.

"They're spinning you as a real ball breaker. How you told Tristan you were cheating on him in front of the entire school. They also make the statue thing into some kind of political statement you were making."

"What sort of political statement am I supposed to be making?"

"It's not really clear, sort of an anticapitalist thing. Down with the man, blah, blah, blah." Kelsie plunked down onto my bed. She pulled the magazine back and flipped through it. "The photo of you is a nasty one. You look like a mouth breather."

"How can they spin me as some sort of rich spoiled heiress on the one hand and an anticapitalist terrorist on the other?"

"Look, these magazines aren't the *New York Times* or *Newsweek*, you know. They aren't known for their journalistic integrity." She flipped a few more pages. "Hey, I hadn't heard this. Did you know these guys had broken up? I always thought she could do better. He always looks like he needs a shower." She turned the magazine to show me a large glossy photo of a rock star and his model girlfriend. Or ex-girlfriend. I pulled the magazine out of her hand. Unwashed musicians were not what I was interested in.

"My family doesn't even have that much money. Mandy's an

heiress. I'm just"—my brain scrambled to find the right term—"like, ordinary rich. Maybe not even rich, just well to do."

"They talk about your vacation home on the lake."

"That's not a vacation home. It's my grandparents' place."

"I know that. I'm telling you what the articles say."

"Articles?" My question came out in a shrill high voice.

"Oh, yeah. There's a version of the same thing in both of these." Kelsie tossed the other magazines onto the bed. "Same picture of you too. That's unfortunate. At least *Star Magazine* used a shot of you from one of the student government meetings where you have your mouth shut."

I flopped facedown onto the bed and buried my face in my pillow. Just when I thought things couldn't get worse. "Has Tristan seen these yet?" I asked, my words muffled by the pillow.

"I called Joel last night when I saw it online and told him to give Tristan the heads-up."

"How exactly did you get the magazines?"

"You know the maid who does the bathrooms? The woman with the ring in her eyebrow that Dean Winston made her take out?" She waited for me to nod that I knew who she was talking about. "Everyone buys their weed from her, so I got her number from one of the girls on the floor and asked her to pick up something legal for a change. Even so, she charged me a hundred bucks to drop them off first thing this morning. Talk about a markup, but what are you going to do?"

"If no one can get off campus, maybe no one will see them," I said.

"I doubt it. I heard Mandy talking about it in the bathroom last night. That's how I knew to look for it. If I can get copies of the magazines, you better believe she can get her hands on copies."

"What is her problem with me?" I rolled over so I could look up at the ceiling.

"Well, first off she's a bitch in general. That's her natural state. Then you add on top of it that you were more popular than her and that you were dating Tristan. She always had a thing for him."

"She likes Tristan?"

"I don't know if she really likes him, but he's the most popular guy here. She likes the idea of them as a couple. I'm not sure she's capable of actual emotion; it's more a thing of how a relationship can benefit her. Dating him would double her star power."

"I don't even know why she's famous to start with. She's stinking rich and pretty. That's it. Oh, and she's willing to flash her hoo-ha to anyone who wants a peek. There's a real claim to fame. She should stick a disco ball between her legs and put down a dance floor, there's so much traffic through there."

"Maybe that's why she vadazzled her snatch last year." Kelsie and I both snorted. Mandy glued Swarovski crystals all over her waxed crotch and then acted surprised when a photographer got pictures. Whoever glues crystals on themselves is clearly doing it with the goal of someone seeing it.

"I still can't believe, with everything happening in the world these days, that my life counts as news."

"Tristan's a big deal. He's news."

"What does that make me?" I asked.

"Collateral damage. If you want to look for the positive, your life drama is most likely helping to support someone on the Evesham staff. It's sort of like sponsoring a kid in a third world country."

"You think the security guard that sold the picture of Mandy sold this story?"

"Someone did. The pictures of you are from campus. The story is all over this place. It might not be the security guard. It could be a maid, or someone from the cooking crew. Then there's the guy you're cleaning with. He'd have an inside track."

"Drew? You think Drew would do this to me? That's so unfair. You think he would do that just because he's from town. Everyone here is always judging everyone else." I felt like pushing Kelsie off the bed.

"Easy. Don't get your panties all knotted up. I'm not saying he did anything. What I said is that he *could* have sold the information. You act like he's your best friend now. Lately everything is all 'Drew says this' and 'Drew does that.' You've known this guy for like a week."

"Why would anyone do this?"

"Why not? Money, most likely. Maybe it's one of those staff people who don't like us because we go to Evesham. You heard about the maid who got canned two years ago because she was caught trying on Stephanie Wild's clothes? They clean our floors, wash our dishes, and make our meals. You have to figure sometimes they look at us and think it's unfair. Heck, maybe it is unfair. It's no wonder there are stories leaked out of here all the time."

I crumpled the cover of one of the glossy magazines. I didn't want to think Drew would do something like this, but I had told him everything that day at Denny's. He'd admitted that he needed to make money for school in the fall. Selling Evesham secrets would be a fast way to make a buck, and he hadn't exactly made a secret of what he thought of Evesham students in general. I think I had hoped it was different with me. My stomach clenched, filling with sour hot acid.

"I can't believe this had to happen now. Things with Tristan were just starting to get better."

"What do you mean?"

"He came to see me last night in the library." I almost laughed when I saw Kelsie's face. "You don't have to look that shocked. We dated for four years, after all. Did you think he'd really never speak to me again?"

"So are you guys getting back together?"

I shrugged. "I don't think he knows what he wants."

"You don't have to make him sound like a child who doesn't

know what to do. The situation really threw him. He trusted you."

I leaned back, surprised at how angry she sounded. "I know. I didn't mean to make it sound like he was doing something wrong. You know how he is. He can't decide what he wants for dinner half the time."

"You always do that. Make snide comments about him. If you don't want to be with him, then don't date him."

"Do I have to do nothing but create poems in his honor? He's a guy. He's got great qualities and he has flaws. Why does everyone assume I don't want to be with Tristan?"

"Oh, I don't know. Hmm, let me think." Kelsie placed her finger on the side of her chin in an exaggerated gesture. "It could be because you were caught kissing some other guy. Or it might be that you make fun of him, or it could be because suddenly you're acting all strange, sneaking off campus, breaking stuff, hanging out with some townie instead of your friends."

I cut her off before she could say any more. "Maybe I'm not hanging out with my usual crowd because just about everyone in it is making me into the campus pariah. Everyone is acting like the fact that they can't get off campus is some great hardship. No one from student council has had anything to do with me, and even you only hang out with me when it works for you."

Kelsie stood up, her face flushing red. "Do you know how many times in the past week I've stood up for you? You act like everyone is blowing you off, but you're blowing them off just as much. You don't come to any of your regular activities. You isolate yourself and then blame us. I gave a hundred bucks to a drug dealer to get you these magazines. What do you want?"

"You're supposed to stand up for me. We're best friends." I reached a hand forward to touch her arm. I couldn't understand how I kept screwing things up with the people that mattered. My dad was mad, my best friend was mad, my boyfriend didn't even know if he wanted to be with me. My best guy friend wanted to be with me, but I didn't know if I wanted to be with him, and someone on campus, possibly the only friend I felt like I had left, was selling out my secrets for a few extra bucks. "I don't want to fight with you, too. I don't want you to be mad. All I was trying to do was explain what's going on for me."

"Whatever. I have to go." Kelsie crossed my room and flung the door open. "You can keep the magazines, and you might want to give some thought to the idea that while stuff is going on for you, the rest of us also have a life."

The door swung shut softly, separating us with a click.

23

I didn't wait for Drew. By now I was becoming a seasoned pro. I didn't need him to hold my hand. I dragged the cart out from the closet and started on the first classroom. If I didn't get into Yale, I could always apply to work as a janitor. Someone had written notes on the white board with a regular marker. I rubbed it harder, but it didn't make a dent. I pulled out the oily cleanser I'd seen Drew use.

"Hey, Prima Donna. I was waiting for you outside," Drew said.

I didn't look behind me and kept my focus on the board. "I want to finish up early if we can. I have a lot of homework."

"That's a shame. I was going to suggest sneaking you out of here after work and doing something fun."

I made a noncommittal noise. My elbow was starting to hurt from the rubbing. I wasn't built for manual labor. I wouldn't make it long term as a janitor. Yet another future opportunity lost to me. "You know what I would consider fun? If you stopped calling me Prima Donna."

"What? It's Italian for 'first lady.'"

"It means 'stuck up,' and you know it." I glared at him over my shoulder.

"Wow. Someone woke up on the wrong side of the mop and bucket today. Better not let anyone see that expression. They're going to start calling you Cruella De Vil on top of America's least favorite heartbreaker."

I dropped the cleanser. "What do you know about that?"

"Just what I read online. You didn't mention that the boyfriend in question was some famous Hollywood star."

"He's not a star. His parents are."

"I don't know. I figure if the people on *Entertainment Tonight* have you on a first name basis, you count as a star."

"What journalists do you know on a first name basis?" I asked, crossing my arms.

Drew raised an eyebrow. "Is this a trick question?"

"Do you find it tricky to answer?" I held my breath while I waited for him to respond. I searched his face, looking to see if I would be able to tell if he was lying. His eyes didn't shift away, and he didn't blush or act like I had caught him. It could mean he had nothing to do with it, or that he was a good liar.

"What are you getting at?" Drew asked.

"Did you sell my story to the magazines?"

Drew took a step back, his face registering shock. "You think I would do that?"

"Someone did."

"Someone is also responsible for that ten-car pileup on the highway, but that also wasn't me. Last I checked, I also didn't start the war overseas, or have anything to do with the banking scandal or global warming. On the whole I've kept my nose pretty clean. If you're looking for a full accounting, I'll admit that when I was twelve I stole a Snickers bar from the local grocery. I've been known to speed in a school zone on occasion, and I've had a few underage beers, but never while driving. My mom would be right that I'm the guy who drinks almost the last of the milk from the carton and then sticks it back in the fridge, and she thinks I should make my bed." Drew stopped, as if he was thinking about it. "I also once dissected my kid sister's teddy bear. She considered it a case of murder, but I honestly wondered what was in there. I'd call it scientific curiosity gone awry. I thought I could put it back together. I was only eight, if that makes a difference."

"When I was that age, I once dug up all the tulip bulbs my mom had buried in the garden. I put them in my closet. I think I thought they might grow in there," I confessed.

"There you go. Neither of us is coming to this situation with clean hands." Drew crossed the room so that our faces were mere inches apart, his eyes locked to mine. "I haven't told anyone what you told me, and I wouldn't. Not for money, not even if they asked me nice."

I felt myself slump with relief. "Okay. I didn't mean to accuse you." All I needed was for him to be mad at me too.

"Nothing wrong with asking. Who else do you think could have done it?"

"One of the security guards sold a picture recently. It might have been her."

"Ah, the Mandy Gallaway scandal."

"You know about it?"

"Are you kidding? The whole staff was pulled into a meeting where we got our asses handed to us. We were all warned that if the administration finds out anyone is selling pictures of the golden children, there will be hell to pay. I'd be surprised if it was anyone on staff after that. I can't think anyone would risk their job over you." Drew pulled out the rag to wipe down the desks. "Is the story a problem? I would think people here would be used to that kind of thing."

"People like Mandy might be used to it, but I prefer to keep my private life private. Half the stuff in that story isn't true anyway."

"Do you really have a bunch of homework you have to do tonight?"

"Yes. I'm sure it seems like all we 'golden children' need to do is manage our media events and look good, but some of us have academic goals too."

"I never doubted you were smart." Drew looked over. "Crazy as all get out, but smart."

I tossed a roll of paper towels at his head, and he ducked.

"Careful. Those are the double thickness towels. Nothing but the best. You could make a baby diaper out of those. You waste supplies, and they take it out of your check."

"Seriously?"

"You think they don't watch our Windex usage? You better believe it. Winston is always convinced people are stealing. He caught a secretary a few years ago taking home a pack of Post-it notes, and you would have thought she was embezzling gold bars instead of some office supplies."

"What were you thinking of doing later?" I asked.

"I thought you had all that homework, not to mention those academic goals."

"I'm not saying I want to go. I'm just interested to know what you're doing. That's what friends do, take an interest."

"What if I won't tell you? Then you'll have to come to find out. It's a surprise."

"I don't like surprises."

"You're missing out. Surprises are what make life interesting."

"Isn't that supposed to be a Chinese curse, that you live in interesting times?"

"I'd take interesting over dull any day."

"So are you going to tell me what you've got planned?"

"Nope. Either you come or you don't. Your choice."

I bustled around emptying the trash cans as if I were too

busy to even consider his plan. Without even glancing over at him, I knew he would be smiling. Smirking, most likely. He was a big smirker. Sneaking off campus was a bad idea. I might have been able to convince Winston once that I was an emotional wreck, but if I got caught again, he wouldn't go so easy on me.

I sprayed the windows with Windex, perhaps a bit less than I might have used in the past, now that I knew there was a cleaning supply Nazi keeping track. I wiped the glass, watching groups of students walking across the quad. I spotted Tristan walking with Kelsie. I raised my arm to wave and catch their attention. Kelsie jabbed Tristan and he pushed her back, and she fell onto her butt on the ice. She threw her head back, and I could see she was laughing. Tristan tried to pull her up, but she used her weight to cause him to fall into the snowbank. I stood frozen, watching them. Tristan got up and tried again to help Kelsie. They were both laughing now. He finally settled for picking Kelsie up like a bag of laundry and throwing her over his shoulder to carry her off. I stepped back slightly so that if they looked at the window they wouldn't see me.

Drew was standing right behind me. He looked past me out the window. "That's Tristan, isn't it?"

I nodded, watching as he and Kelsie headed back toward the dorms.

"Who's with him?" Drew asked.

"Her name's Kelsie. She's my best friend." I pinned Drew in place with my expression, stopping him before he could say anything. "The two of them are friends too. They're always joking around like that. Tristan says Kelsie's the annoying younger sister that he never wanted."

"Fair enough." Drew turned away to go back to the mopping.

I kept an eye out the window, waiting to see if I would spot them again. "I'll go with you after work," I said suddenly. "I feel like a surprise."

24

I swallowed hard to keep myself from throwing up. I knew I didn't like surprises. I had assumed Drew would have planned some sort of physical activity. Something that he thought would scare me. Bungee jumping off a bridge, ski jumping, or walking over hot coals. Now I realized there was something worse than putting myself in a life-and-death situation.

Karaoke.

A woman on the stage was singing some Top 40 song. The sound coming out of her was what I imagined would come out of livestock if you hooked them up to a car battery. More people would have been laughing at her, except she was doing this bump and grind number that was too hard-core for most porn movies, so the men in the audience were distracted. The bar wasn't like anyplace I'd been before. I'd been to a few of the nightclubs in LA with Tristan, but they were all red-rope affairs where you didn't get into the building if you weren't already on the A-list. This place looked to be a bit less discriminating. There were a few people in the back of the room that I suspected didn't even have a pulse. They appeared to be passed out in their beers. While the clubs I'd been to spent millions on décor and imported glass and marble from Europe, this place had a décor that seemed to be themed around plug-in beer signs.

I shifted in the seat. My glass of Diet Coke was making a puddle of condensation on the table in front of me. Drew jammed another nacho into his mouth. He'd ordered them with triple jalapeño peppers. It was a wonder his mouth didn't start shooting flames. He pushed the laminated pages back over to me.

"You still haven't picked a song," he said with salsa in his teeth.

"I'm not sure there's anything I like." I held the song list between two fingers. There was something sticky on the pages. I had no desire to even think what it might be.

"There's over two hundred songs on there. You can't find anything? I'm all for being discriminating, but at some point it becomes picky."

"I'm not sure I should be singing at all. My throat's been a bit sore. I might be coming down with something." I held my hand to my throat and tried to look wan.

Drew laughed. "Do not go into a life of crime. You suck at lying. You're not sick, and your throat is fine. Either you pick a song or I pick a song for you. If you want to pick a duet, I'll do it with you if you're too nervous to be up there by yourself. Or I could pick something super-embarrassing and sing it to you."

I slouched down in my seat, pouting. I pulled the list over and began looking through it again. Most of the duets were love songs. No way was I going to stand up in that bar and sing "Endless Love" with Drew.

"I don't see why I have to do a song at all. Why can't we just watch other people sing? That's fun." I gestured to the group of guys who had taken the stage and were belting out "You Shook Me All Night Long" by AC/DC. One guy was attempting to use his leg as a guitar. He fell over a stool, but popped right back up.

"Don't you want to be a part of things?" Drew's hand tapped the table to the beat of the music.

"Not if being a part of things means humiliating myself."

"There are two kinds of people in this world. People who are a part of what happens and people who sit back and watch other people make it happen. Life isn't supposed to be a spectator sport. It's supposed to be messy." Drew took my hand and leaned closer. His hands were rough with calluses. "Tell me the truth. When you were a kid, did you always color inside the lines?"

I went to pull my hand away, but he held it tighter. His hands were warm. I looked around to see if anyone noticed us touching. With my luck there would be some magazine reporter in the bar who would take a picture. "Coloring in the lines is the whole point. That's why they have lines," I said.

"That's where you're wrong. The lines are there just to hold you in. Like a prison. Think what you might have created if there hadn't been any lines. To quote my friend Thoreau: 'I wanted to live deep and suck out all the marrow of life, . . . to put to rout all that was not life . . . and not, when I came to die, discover that I had not lived.' Now, there was a guy who didn't color in the lines." Drew raised his glass to the ceiling as if to salute Thoreau, dropping my hand. He was able to quote poets. There was no end of random information he knew.

"I'm not sure we should be taking life advice from him. Thoreau lived in the woods, like some kind of crazy hermit," I said.

"Call him crazy if you want, but the guy is immortal because of what he did. He took risks. Did you know he was part of the Underground Railroad that helped sneak slaves north toward freedom? This was a guy who marched to the beat of his own drum. How many line followers are immortal?"

"How many people who don't stay in the lines cross into oncoming traffic and end up getting hit by a car?" I countered. This was something I knew from personal experience.

Drew rolled his eyes. "Singing in public isn't going to kill you. It won't even maim you. The only thing that's going to get bruised is your ego." Drew pulled the song list back over to his side of the table. He used the pencil on the table to scribble a song number on a sheet of paper. He pulled me up from my chair. "There you go. Now it's done. Come on. We're up."

"Wait, what song did you pick?"

"It's a surprise. I know how you love surprises." Drew winked. He pulled me by the arm toward the stage, handing our slip of paper over to the DJ running the music.

"What if I don't know the words?" I dragged my feet, trying to slow our process.

"That's why they have them on the TV." Drew motioned to the small screen to the side of the stage. "You haven't been going to that fancy school for this long without learning to read. All you have to do is follow along. Now, once we get going, I expect you to belt it out."

The DJ called our names, and Drew jumped up onto the stage as if he couldn't wait. He handed me a microphone and took one for himself. A few people in the crowd hooted while we waited to start. I prayed that there would be some kind of natural disaster. A small earthquake would work, anything that would stop what was about to happen. All I needed was for the ground to split open and swallow me alive. It would also work if Drew were swallowed alive. Either option was fine with me.

The music started. Drew had picked "What a Wonderful World" by Louis Armstrong. I'd heard the song before, but I had to follow the lyrics on the TV to sing along. At least it wasn't as bad as some things he could have chosen. Looking out at the audience made me feel like I was going to pass out, so I focused on a flashing Budweiser sign at the back of the room. Drew stood next to me, throwing his arm around me so that we could sway in tandem back and forth for the final verse. Drew motioned to the crowd, and they yelled along with us, "I think to myself, what a wonderful world!"

Everyone cheered for us when we were done. Drew held my hand, and we bowed to the audience. Drew waved to the people in the back. I was starting to think I was going to have to drag him off the stage. I found myself smiling and taking a few extra bows while pulling him toward the stairs.

When we sat back down, some people a few tables over bought us a round of Cokes. Drew leaned back in his chair and put his feet up on the chair next to me.

"Admit it. You had fun." He shook his finger at me.

"It wasn't as bad as I thought it might be."

"Not bad?" Drew waved off my comments. "Coming from you that's practically a giddy endorsement."

"Unlike you, I'm not a karaoke pro. It would take more than one song to make me feel comfortable."

"I'm not a pro. I've never done this before just now."

The chip I was eating fell out of my mouth. "What do you mean?"

"I mean I've never done it. I saw the flyer at the Laundromat that they do karaoke here, and it sounded like fun." Drew noticed my expression. "You've heard of Laundromats, right? It's where the average people go to air their dirty laundry, instead of in tabloid magazines."

I looked down my nose at him. "Ha, ha. Yes, I've heard of Laundromats. I'm just surprised you haven't done this before.

You jumped up there like the stage was your second home."

"I'm a big believer in faking it until you make it. If you're going to do something, you can't always sidle up to it. You have to jump in with both feet."

"No guts, no glory, huh? Not everyone has that kind of courage. Some of us have a normal sense of fear."

"You know what courage is, don't you? It's not a lack of fear. It's being scared and doing it anyway." Drew put his feet back on the floor and leaned forward. "Like asking your friend what's up with her and Tristan, instead of letting it eat you up inside."

I choked on my Diet Coke. "Now you've lost your mind. There's nothing going on between them."

"You don't need to convince me. You're the one bothered by it."

"I'm not bothered by it," I yelled. The people at the tables near us turned to see what was going on. Hanging out with Drew was turning me into one of those people who hangs out in cheap bars and has screaming matches in public. I pressed my mouth into a smile, lowered my voice, and repeated myself through clenched teeth. "I'm not bothered."

"I can see that." Drew pulled the straw out of his glass and chugged his Coke.

"I'm not."

"Okay. You're not. My mistake." Drew took another long drink. "All I'm saying is that life is too short to sit back and wait to see what happens, what everyone else decides. You're in charge of your own life. If your dad is ticking you off, then you should tell him. If you don't want to see Tristan anymore, then break up with him. If you think your friend is dating your boyfriend, then ask her."

I shook my head. "You're reading too much be-all-you-can-be poetry. That, or all that sucking the marrow out of life has resulted in an oxygen shortage. It's not that simple. In polite society we don't always do whatever comes into our head." I glanced down at my watch. "I should get back. I need to sneak back into my room before eleven."

Drew shrugged and pulled his coat on. I followed him out into the parking lot. The silence seemed jarring after the loud music in the bar. I could hear the squeak of my shoes in the fresh snow.

"I suppose you always do what you want," I said. "You go out and seize every day like some sort of motivational speaker."

Drew pulled on my jacket to make me stop. "If you don't seize the opportunity, how do you know what will happen? Sometimes you have to take the chance."

I started to disagree with him, but Drew leaned in and kissed me. Not a friendly peck on the cheek, but a full-on tongue-in-my-mouth face-sucking kiss. My mind went completely blank. Before Tristan the only person I had kissed was Wilbur Trent in seventh grade. Wilber sat behind me in class, and his mom had invited me to his birthday party, where he kissed me in the living room while we were supposed to be watching a movie. He had tasted a bit like the Juicy Fruit gum he was always chewing. There was no tongue with Wilbur. That summer his dad was transferred to Colorado and our young love affair never had another chance. Once at Evesham, I started dating Tristan the fall of freshman year and hadn't kissed another soul until Joel had planted one on me that night by the statue. Now Drew was kissing me out of nowhere. I couldn't tell what was going on in my life that suddenly people felt the urge to kiss me without being invited. I must have been giving off some kind of hormone scent that made people think I was easy. I could feel the sharp brush of Drew's stubble as it ground against my face. He pulled back and stared at me. I knew he was waiting for me to say something. I waited for the words to form, but my brain was blank.

I slapped him hard across the face. The crack of my hand against his skin sounded unnaturally loud in the quiet parking lot. Drew's face went bright red in the perfect shape of my hand.

"Well, that answers that question," Drew said.

"How dare you." I forced myself to take a deep breath and calm down. "I don't know what gave you the idea that that was something I wanted. I've enjoyed getting to know you, and I appreciate all the help you've given me over the past few weeks, but I don't have those sort of feelings." I hoped he wouldn't leave me in the parking lot, but what did he expect? You can't just kiss people.

"Easy, Prima Donna. It was a kiss. It wasn't an unending declaration of love or a marriage proposal. I took a chance, and not all chances can turn out as good as karaoke."

I didn't know if I should be relieved that he wasn't upset, or ticked that he was comparing kissing me to karaoke. "What do we do now?" I asked.

"Well, if we're going to get you back to the dorm on time, we should leave." Drew climbed into the truck. I watched my exhaled breath fog in the cold air. For someone who was always advocating that people should talk about things, he'd picked a fine time to go silent. I climbed into the passenger seat and slammed the door. Men.

We drove back to campus in silence. Drew pulled the truck to the side of the road behind the administration building. He got out and trudged up to the stone wall that circled the campus.

"You coming?"

If he thought playing it cool was going to upset me, he was wrong. I'd perfected acting like nothing was wrong for a good part of my life. I stomped through the deep snow. Drew bent over and cupped his hands. I stepped into his palm, and he hefted me up onto the wall. I sat on top and spun my legs around so that I could drop onto the campus side.

"Thanks for bringing me back to campus," I said. I dropped to the ground, the pile of snow cushioning my fall. I took a quick glance around to make sure no one had seen me.

"Hey, Hailey?" Drew's voice drifted over the wall.

I considered pretending that I hadn't heard him and just walking away, but I couldn't do it. "Yeah," I called back softly.

"I still think it's a wonderful world."

25

Joel was sitting outside my door in the dorm hallway working on his math homework when I got back. I wondered how long he'd been waiting. When he saw me, he stood.

"Where were you?"

"Studying," I said, before I realized I didn't have any books or notes with me. Joel looked me up and down, noting the clumps of snow on my socks. "I took a walk to clear my head."

"Through the snow?"

"It's winter. Sort of hard to avoid the snow. Besides, I like fresh air." I unlocked my door and went in, leaving the door swinging behind me. Evesham allowed people of the opposite sex to visit the dorms, but you had to leave the door open. It was supposed to prevent people from having sex. Clearly the administration didn't have the imagination that the student body did. Evesham was full of places where couples could hook up. "What's up?" I asked, sitting down on my bed so I could pull my wet socks off. My legs were red from the cold. The bright red skin made me think of Drew's face. I shoved that image out of my head. I wasn't prepared to deal with Drew right now. I was having a hard enough time figuring out what to say to Joel. I was suddenly aware we hadn't spent much time in each other's company by ourselves since the whole statue incident.

"I tried to call you, but you didn't pick up your phone," Joel said. "You're supposed to keep it on so that I can get in touch with you. I'm responsible for making sure you're meeting the conditions of your punishment."

"I didn't think about it." I shrugged.

"I needed to talk with you about your punishment."

"That's good. I needed to talk to you, too."

"Dean Winston is getting flack from people's parents about the restriction rules."

"He can always decide to lift it." I pulled on a pair of hot pink fleece socks that my grandma had given me for Christmas last year. I wiggled my toes to get the blood moving.

"He isn't going to give in," Joel said.

"If you're worried that I'm going to tell on you, I'm not. It's up to him what he chooses to do about that. He can keep me on restriction for the rest of the year if he wants."

"I feel bad," Joel said.

I pushed down a wave of annoyance. I couldn't remember if Joel had always been this passive or if this was something new.

Wasn't it enough that I was the one in trouble? Did I also have to make him feel okay about it? I couldn't imagine Drew ever talking about how he felt bad. If he felt bad, he would *do* something, not just talk about it.

"If you want, you can help me out with something else," I said. "I need you to get me off the cleaning crew. Isn't there something else I can do? Wash dishes in the café? Maybe shelve books in the library? I like the library."

"I don't think Winston's going to change his mind about the cleaning. I think he would see the library as too easy."

"Can you get me assigned to work with someone else?" I avoided Joel's eyes. "That guy, Drew . . . He and I aren't getting along. I don't want to work with him anymore." It wasn't that I disliked Drew, but I had more awkward friend-kissing situations than I could handle already.

"How well do you have to get along? You're cleaning classrooms. I didn't figure the two of you would become friends or anything."

"He hit on me, okay?" My voice came out flat. "It's a bit awkward working with him." I stood up and began bustling around my desk. I stacked my books and folders back in order. I'd forgotten about an essay due for English. I was going to be stuck staying up late.

"Oh." Joel sat staring at his math book. "I can see what I can do. It's completely inappropriate for him to try anything with a student. He's asking for trouble. You would think he would know enough not to take advantage of the situation." He touched the back of my hand.

My hand froze in place, and then I yanked it back to dig through my backpack, looking for my book. "It's not that he's creepy or anything. I don't want to get him fired. It's not that big a deal. It's just uncomfortable. He likes me and I don't like him. That's all." I pulled the book out and flopped into my desk chair. "Like, today, he said this bizarre thing trying to make me jealous. Get this. He said he thought Tristan and Kelsie were seeing each other." I snorted to show how absurd I thought the whole thing was. "Talk about a transparent bid to get my attention."

Joel was silent. His face was frozen as if I were pointing a pistol at his head instead of just looking at him. His Adam's apple was bouncing up and down. My stomach sank to the floor.

"What's going on?" I whispered.

"It's not really my place to say anything." Joel wiped his hands on his pants.

"Don't pull that 'I'm neutral' act with me." I crossed the room in two steps and grabbed hold of Joel's sweater. I was prepared to shake the truth out of him if I had to. "Are they a couple?" I held the sleeve tighter in case he had any plans of making a run for it.

"I don't know." He held up his hand as if he thought I might hit him. "I swear, I don't know. Right after everything went down, Kelsie was around a lot. More than usual, or maybe it seemed like more because you weren't there too. Tristan was really upset, and, I don't know. They've been hanging out. Doing stuff just the two of them. You know Kelsie's always had a case of hero worship for him."

"And Tristan?"

"I think he likes that Kelsie likes him. She's always telling him how great he is and building him up," Joel said.

I let go of Joel's sweater. "I don't get it. I never even imagined the two of them together." I pushed down a feeling in my gut that I had imagined it before, that some part of me had suspected for a while.

"They have a lot in common, you know. Kelsie wants to go into acting, and Tristan's a part of that world, with his folks and all." Joel shrugged as if he were overcome by the destiny that was pulling Kelsie and Tristan together.

"That's a lot in common? That's one thing. What about the fact that Kelsie's a vegetarian and Tristan's favorite food is a rare steak? He never met a living animal that he wouldn't kill and grill. He would eat a kitten burger if it came with pickles. Or how about the fact that Kelsie can spend hours debating the shape of her eyebrows and Tristan hates that high maintenance stuff? Oh, wait. I forgot they both have a connection to acting." I smacked myself in the forehead. "How stupid of me not to see that they're meant for each other. I feel so foolish having stood in the way of true love all this time."

I realized I was crying, which made me mad. I dragged my sleeve across my face to wipe away the tears.

Joel touched my shoulder. "Don't be upset."

"I'm not upset!" My voice snagged in my throat, giving a hiccup sob. The tears came faster. Joel put his arm around me and had me sit on the bed. He knelt on the floor in front of me. Tristan and Kelsie didn't have much in common, but Joel and I did. We were both overachievers, we liked to watch the news and debate the issues, and we both preferred books versus anything on TV. In theory he and I were perfectly matched, but I'd never thought of him that way before that night. Now I couldn't tell if I was confused because I did like him, or that I liked that he liked me. Maybe I was only afraid of being left alone, especially if Tristan was picking Kelsie.

"I don't think Kelsie or Tristan want you to be hurt," Joel said.

"They should have told me. I know I'm in no position to be angry with Tristan, given what happened, but sneaking around means they think it's wrong too. If Kelsie thought dating Tristan was fine, she would have said something. She and I are supposed to be best friends."

"She's hurt that you didn't tell her who you were kissing that night." He cut me off before I could protest. "I know why you didn't tell her, but she doesn't understand. Neither of them knew what to say, so they didn't say anything."

I sniffed. My nose was running. "Why didn't you tell me? You could have warned me. I shouldn't have had to hear that from Drew."

Joel took both of my hands in his. He was on his knees, and I had the sudden fear he was going to propose.

"You're right. I should have told you, but it was complicated. What happened between us that night? It wasn't an accident. I've been in love with you for a long time. I should have told you about Tristan and Kelsie, but I think part of me wanted them to get together. I didn't want to get in the way of it. I hoped that if they were a couple, you wouldn't spend any more time worrying about him. I figured you wouldn't feel bogged down with guilt. That maybe you would see me with new eyes."

My heart sped up. I wanted to pick up my wet socks from the floor and shove them into Joel's mouth to keep him from saying anything else. "We've been friends a long time," I said, trying to remind him. Weren't the best relationships supposed to be based on friendship? Was that enough?

"You know freshman year? I liked you even then. I remember how your dad had ordered the wrong size uniform for you. Those first few weeks you were always having to hitch your skirt back up and roll the sleeves on your sweater up until your new uniform arrived."

"You never said anything to me. You never acted like you liked me," I said.

"The first time I got up the guts to talk to you, you asked about Tristan, my roommate."

I flinched. "Sorry."

"Can't say I blame you. Tristan was already, you know, Tristan, and I was such a dork back then. I weighed, like, eighty pounds. Remember how everyone called me the beanpole?"

I smiled, but if I had been honest, I would have told Joel that I didn't have a lot of memories of him from freshman year. I'd been so homesick at first. I'd felt lost among all these people who seemed totally comfortable living without their parents. I hadn't wanted to screw anything up, and then suddenly in the middle of all of that there was Tristan. He always seemed so confident and was so good-looking. Tristan always teased me about how hard to get I'd been in those first few weeks, but I hadn't been playing at anything. It had never occurred to me that he would actually like me. The fact that he'd been flirting with me had sailed right over my head.

"I never knew," I said. "You never said anything, even after what happened at the statue."

"I guess I hoped you'd realize it wasn't an accident. Then when you didn't, I didn't want to push things. I hoped that eventually you would look around and notice me." Joel shrugged. "I think I was hoping you'd think it was destiny."

"You can't do that. You can't sit back and wait for life to happen to you. You should have said something." As the words came out of my mouth, an image of Drew flashed into my mind. I touched my lips lightly as if I expected to feel the burn of his mouth on mine.

"I couldn't do that. Not to Tristan. What was I going to say, 'Hey, guess what? I have a crush on your girlfriend.' I always figured you guys would eventually break up and then after a decent amount of time I would step in. Who would have thought you guys would stay together for all of high school?"

The idea that Joel had been spending the past four years just waiting for something to happen made me sad.

"So when Kelsie and Tristan got together, you didn't mind at all. It must have looked like your opportunity was finally here."

"I swear I never planned it." Joel raised his hand as if he were taking the Boy Scout pledge. Joel was a good guy. I suspected he was right. He never would have done anything to try to get a chance with me. He would have sat back and waited forever if he needed to. He wouldn't have wanted to upset anyone.

"Hailey, I love you. I've loved you for a long time. I know this must seem sudden to you, but it's not. You're right. We have been friends for years. Maybe now we can see if it might grow into something more."

"You don't love me," I said, pulling my hands back, suddenly sure.

"How can you say that?"

"If you loved me, you would have taken the chance. You would have risked having everything go wrong because the slim chance that it might go right would have been enough to make it worth it. Love is risky."

Joel leaned back on his heels. He was like one of those giant inflatable parade balloons that had sprung a leak. "You want to be with Tristan," he said.

I sighed. "Not everything is a competition between the two

of you. I thought I wanted to be with Tristan, but I don't know. Maybe I wanted to be with Tristan because it's easy." I shrugged. "It might not even be up to me. It sounds like he and Kelsie are an item now."

"I bet he would drop her if he knew you guys could work it out."

"Then, that's a shame. Kelsie deserves better than that." I touched the side of Joel's face. "You do too. You deserve someone who's crazy about you."

"But that's not you," he said, his eyes filling up.

"No, it's not me."

26

I stared at my copy of *The Count of Monte Cristo*. For some reason writing an essay for English on the effects of betrayal seemed a bit too close to home. I considered calling Kelsie, but I wasn't sure how to start the conversation. How do you ask your best friend if she's seeing your boyfriend?

Kelsie and I hadn't become friends right away at Evesham. I'd thought she was too wild. Freshman year I was known for having color-coded file folders that matched my notebooks, and she was known for having the largest collection of lip gloss. She'd gotten in trouble at Halloween for wearing a cat costume to the masquerade party that would have made a stripper blush. She hung with the party crowd, and I hung with the nerds.

Kelsie and I had been assigned to do a project together for biology. She refused to touch the worm we were supposed to dissect, on ethical grounds. She was already a member of PETA and threatened that if our teacher made her touch "the innocent wildlife victim," then she would arrange a protest march that would shut down the science wing. Our teacher decided that I would handle the dissection portion of the project and Kelsie would write up our results. I could tell ten minutes into the project that if I wanted to keep up my A average, I was going to have to write the paper too. I based this on the fact that Kelsie wasn't interested in writing down anything I was doing with our worm. She was more interested in creating a chart that listed the calorie burn and fitness potential for a range of activities, so that she could get the maximum burn in the least amount of time.

"It's genetics, you know. My grandmother was Italian, which makes me predisposed to plump up. It's all the carbs." Kelsie shook her head as if she couldn't believe this cruel twist of fate.

"I'm pretty sure this part of the worm is the esophagus," I said, pointing and trying to pull her attention back to what we were supposed to be doing.

Kelsie didn't even look over into the tray. "You know the other issue I have to worry about? Facial hair. Italian women are very prone to those long black chin hairs." She wiggled her fingers at the end of her chin as if to demonstrate how all the hair would look waving in the wind.

"I didn't know that," I said. If I thought I was going to have a beard, I wouldn't tell anyone. I wasn't sure if I was supposed to be impressed or repulsed.

"It's true. You can tell I'm going to be hairy by looking at my eyebrows." Kelsie pointed with a perfectly manicured finger to her face.

I inspected them, leaning in close to get a better look. "They look fine to me."

"Well, of course they do. Do you think I would show up in public unless I'd been waxed? I've been plucking since I was ten. I remove enough hair per week to make wigs for at least two kids with cancer."

"Wow." I looked back at our worm corpse.

"I'm guessing you don't have facial hair issues, huh? Nordic heritage?"

"Me? No. My family's originally from Ireland." I touched my eyebrows with one latex-covered finger.

"You're lucky. You can't beat good genes. No wonder Tristan likes you."

I chopped our worm in two, shocked at what she said.

"Are we supposed to make two worms?" Kelsie asked, leaning in.

"Why would you say Tristan likes me?" My voice was high and a bit screechy. I whirled around to make sure he was still sitting across the room and hadn't heard what she said. He looked up from his worm tray and smiled. I spun back in case he thought I was staring at him.

"What's the matter? He's cute. I wish someone like that liked me," Kelsie said.

"He doesn't like me." I pushed the worm ends back together,

hoping either the worm would spontaneously heal itself or our teacher wouldn't notice what I'd done. "He's just nice."

"Are you blind?" Kelsie tapped me on the back of the hand. "You might know science, but I know boys. He's been flirting with you."

I casually scratched my back so I could turn enough to have Tristan in my view again. He was still glancing toward our table. I backed up quickly, and my lab chair fell over, making a loud clang on the tile floor. Our science teacher scowled. She wasn't fond of clowning around in her lab.

"He's staring at me," I whispered out of the side of my mouth to Kelsie. "What do I do?"

Kelsie smiled. "You're in luck. In addition to being plump, and the chin hair thing, Italians are naturals with love and romance. I can totally help you. Romeo and Juliet were Italian, you know."

I thought about telling her that Romeo and Juliet were created by Shakespeare, who was British, but I decided I wanted her advice more than I wanted to make a point.

Her advice worked too. It wasn't hard advice to follow. It consisted mostly of meeting his eyes instead of looking away, flipping my hair around like I was having some kind of seizure, and wearing lower-cut shirts. By the end of that week Tristan and I went from shameless flirting in the cafeteria, to talking after class, to kissing while hidden in the stacks of the library, to being a full-fledged established couple. In addition to gaining a boyfriend, I'd gained a best friend. Kelsie and I hadn't been separated since that time.

Now I needed to know what to do, and the person I usually went to for advice was the one person I couldn't ask.

I looked at my watch. It was an hour earlier in Chicago; it wasn't *that* late. No one would consider it the middle of the night. Weren't parents supposed to be the ones we went to when there was trouble? Adults were always telling us that we should go to them. I pulled my cell out of my bag and hit the number before I had time to overthink the situation. He picked up the phone before it finished ringing the first time.

"I thought we said we wouldn't talk again until morning," my dad purred into the phone.

"Dad?"

"Hailey?" His purr was gone. "What's wrong? Are you okay?" He gasped slightly. "Your not in jail, are you?"

"No, I'm not in jail." I couldn't keep the annoyance out of my voice. Jail? Really? I'd been in trouble exactly twice in my high school career, and because I called at ten p.m. the first thing that came into his mind was that I must have been picked up by the cops?

"Why are you calling?"

"Who did you think was calling?" I narrowed my eyes as if I could see through the cell phone into my dad's eyes.

"I'm not having this conversation with you now."

My heart stopped. My dad was dating someone. "You have a

girlfriend?" Logically I knew there was always the chance that my dad would see someone at some point. It wasn't that I expected him to be alone forever with a shrine to my mom above the gas fireplace in the living room, but he'd never said anything. This felt sneaky and wrong.

My dad sighed. "This isn't something I planned to talk about on the phone."

I held off from pointing out that since he was always out of town and we never saw each other, the phone was pretty much our only option. Maybe he'd been planning to save this discussion for graduation, or maybe he'd never planned to tell me at all. There'd been a lot of that going on in my life lately.

"I've been seeing someone. Her name is Linda." His voice sounded nervous. "She works with me. I think you'll like her. She's smart and funny. She's an engineer. I thought maybe you could meet her this summer up at Grandma's."

"Huh." I kicked at the floor with my foot. "How do you know you'll still be dating her in the summer?"

"I knew you wouldn't be happy about this. Seeing Linda doesn't change how I feel about your mom."

"How does Linda feel about you being gone all summer?"

There was silence on the phone. "Linda will be in London with me. The project over there is hers."

My throat narrowed. "Linda's project is in London." I felt my breath come low and shallow. "That's why you changed our summer plans. You wanted to go with your girlfriend on vacation." My voice stretched out the word "girlfriend," making it sound slimy.

"It isn't that straightforward."

"All I wanted for graduation was to spend the summer with you. You told me we could, and you let me plan a party for all my friends."

"I know canceling your party was a disappointment, but this workshop in England is very important. I would hope you could understand that, especially given your age. You're not a child."

"Well, I'm glad you noticed I'm growing up. And for the record, it wasn't some little party; it was a chance for me to spend one last time with my friends before we all go our separate ways. That might not seem like a big deal to you, but these people have been my family for the past four years. You know, family, what you used to be a part of."

"This isn't like you. You've become belligerent and angry. It's not becoming. I don't know what's gotten into you."

"Then, ask me! It's not a big secret. I was calling to tell you. I don't even know who I am anymore. I'm not sure what I want. I feel like you don't want me in your life. Tristan and I broke up. Kelsie, who's supposed to be my best friend, is dating Tristan on the sly. Joel likes me, which is totally awkward, because we're supposed to be friends. Then there's this other guy, who sort of drives me nuts, but then I kinda like him at the same time." I took a deep breath, but before I could go on, my dad cut me off.

"This is a hard time, with graduation coming and all. I'll call

Dean Winston tomorrow and arrange for you to talk to someone. They must have a counselor there given what they charge."

"I don't want to talk to Ms. Sullivan. I want to talk to you."

"Girl problems aren't my thing. If your mom were here, she'd know the right thing to say."

"There isn't a right thing, Dad."

"Now, look, I'm going to call the school tomorrow, and we can talk again later, when you're not so upset. Or you could give your grandma a call. She'd love a long chat with you."

"I don't want to talk later, I want to talk now, and I want to talk to you." I hated how my voice sounded whiny.

"Take care of yourself, pumpkin. You know I love you."

"Dad, wait." I hated these conversations on the phone.

"Sleep tight." He clicked the phone off.

My dad hung up on me. He *hung up* on me. Maybe he thought because he said he loved me before he did it that it wouldn't count, but a hang up is a hang up. I might only be seventeen, but I know a hang up when it happens.

I picked up the phone to call him back. My finger hovered over the button. What if he didn't pick up? He would glance at the call display this time. He would know who was on the line. I chewed on my thumbnail. It would almost be worse if he did pick up and did the platitudes thing where he told me how everything was fine without actually listening to a word I said and then told me to call someone else.

I bet he was on the phone talking to Linda already, telling her how hard it was for him to deal with a difficult teenage daughter. Maybe London Linda was offering to come over and rub all that tension out of his back. She'd giggle and tell him how she was a real handful when she was my age. He'd pull her into his lap and say she was still a handful.

Gag.

I paced back and forth in my room. I'd taken psychology class. I knew that my dad had a hard time dealing with me because I reminded him of my mom. Heck, what was it Drew had said? We all had our issues. He was still my dad. Just because it was hard didn't give him an excuse to bail out. My mom had died, but my dad was just as absent from my life. I might as well have been an orphan.

I couldn't believe he had chosen going to London with his new girlfriend over spending the summer with me. After he'd promised! Of course, for all I knew, Linda wasn't a new girl-friend. He could have been dating her since I started at Evesham. I couldn't decide what was worse, that he had a girlfriend he'd kept secret for years or that he was chucking our plans over some-one he'd met only a few months ago. I pictured him and Linda walking through the London streets. Maybe she liked antiques like my mom.

My vision narrowed to a small dot. He didn't want to hear what I had to say, but if I was in his face, he wouldn't be able to hang up. He'd have to listen to me then. It might not change what was going to happen. Most likely he'd still go to London, and if I was honest, I wasn't sure I even wanted to spend the summer with him anymore. What I did know for sure is that I wasn't going to sit back and wait for the chance to tell him how I felt.

I flipped open my laptop.

I was going to Chicago.

27

I was awake before my alarm even went off at five forty-five. I'd stayed up late last night getting everything together, but I was still humming with adrenaline, so I didn't even feel tired. I wanted to be ready to go as soon as the clock rolled over to six. My credit card had just enough left on the limit to cover the ticket and cab fair to my dad's place. I'd packed a small duffel bag to take with me. I wouldn't need much. I wasn't planning to stay for long.

I'd struggled with what to do about everyone at school. When I didn't show up in class, someone would come looking for me. I didn't want them to think I'd gone missing and there was some mystery to be solved. There was nothing that CNN and the tabloids loved more than a missing white girl. I'd have Nancy Grace all over my butt before the day was out. I needed to leave a note so people would know I was okay, but not give them any information so they could find me. It took me a while to come up with the perfect wording. The note was pinned to my bed so it would be found when they came to look for me.

Once I was over the fence, I'd call Drew and see if he would pick me up and drive me to the airport. There was the chance he wouldn't talk to me after what had happened, but I was counting on him sticking with playing it cool. If he wouldn't come, I'd have to walk. I didn't want to do that, but I would if I had to. There was only one hitch in the plan. I needed my passport.

Airline security required photo identification. I'd searched everywhere for my driver's license. I didn't have a car at Evesham, so I almost never needed my license. The last time I could remember having it was Christmas, when I'd used it to drive to the mall with my grandma. I had a sinking feeling that it was still in the dress coat that I'd worn over the Christmas holidays. The coat that would be hanging in my grandparents' front hall closet. I wasn't willing to wait for my grandparents to FedEx me my license, not to mention that they would want to know why I needed it right now. My only other option was my passport. There was no way an airline was going to let me through security with only my school ID.

Evesham had kept our passports in the administration building ever since two juniors ran off for an elicit weekend in Paris a few years ago. This is the problem with people having a lot of money but not always a lot of sense. People could still get into a lot of trouble, but with our passports locked up, I guess the theory was that we wouldn't get too far. Dean Winston's secretary had them in a giant lateral file cabinet behind her desk. The janitorial staff started unlocking buildings on campus at six a.m., but in most cases staff and faculty didn't start the day until closer to seven or seven thirty. All I needed to do was get into the building and up to Winston's office, liberate my passport, and get out before anyone knew what I'd done.

I pulled on sweats and my sneakers. My story if anyone saw me wandering around campus this early was that I'd wanted to go for a run. It would still be a bit odd. This time of year most people either ran on the treadmills in the fitness center or at the track in the gym, but it was the best story I could come up with.

I shut my door behind me and passed a couple of girls in their bathrobes shuffling their way to the bathroom. I crept downstairs and saw Ms. Estes in the lobby. I stopped and did some exaggerated stretches trying to look fit and sporty. I bounced on the balls of my feet and swung my arms around to get the blood moving. I jogged in place for a beat, and then left the building. I could feel her eyes on my back. There wasn't anything she could say; at six a.m. I wasn't breaking any rules by leaving. I jogged down the path in case she was still watching, and waited until I had rounded the corner of the dorm before I stopped running and headed off across the quad to the administration building.

The front door to the administration building clicked open. The hallway was lit, but the doors to most of the offices were closed. My wet sneakers made a loud squeaking noise on the tile floor. It seemed like with each step my shoes were screaming out *I'm doing something I shouldn't!*

I ran up the stairs toward Winston's outer office. The only person I saw was one of the maids using a floor buffer way down the hall. She didn't even look up when I went past. I tapped lightly on the door in case his secretary had come in early. The door creaked open a few inches. I peeked my head inside. Winston's private office door across the room was closed, and I was willing to bet it was locked, too. The outer office had two sofas where visiting parents or important people could wait. Directly outside Winston's office were two hard-backed chairs and a bench where those of us in trouble were relegated to wait for our fate. The secretary's desk was almost directly in the center of the office, with the file cabinet right behind it. I took a few steps forward. My heart was beating fast. Up until this point I would still have been able to make an excuse as to what I was doing there, but soon there would be no amount of explanations that would make things okay. My hands were shaking. I either had to take the plunge or go back to the dorm and forget the entire idea.

I let my mind slip back to the phone call with my dad the night before, and that was all the motivation I needed. I wasn't done with that conversation. I crossed the rest of the way to the file cabinet. I pulled on the center drawer labeled *G* through *K*. I yanked harder. It was locked. I wanted to scream from frustration. I wondered how hard it would be to pick the lock. Growing up, I'd taken hundreds of courses in gymnastics, ice-skating, crafts, and swim lessons, but I'd never learned anything really useful like lock picking. If I ever had kids, they wouldn't waste their time gluing Popsicle sticks together. I'd make them learn skills that would come in handy later in life. I kicked the cabinet, in case the drawer might fly open like in the movies. Nope. I'd come this far, and I'd been beaten by a two-dollar lock. My brain scrambled to think of a way around the problem; maybe I wouldn't need my passport. I tried to think if there would be any way to sneak onto the plane without my photo ID, but with my luck I'd be caught and accused of being a terrorist.

I stood there feeling defeated. Unless I was willing to start whacking away at the cabinet with a stapler, I was screwed. I took a couple steps toward the door. I'd have to go back to the dorm and take my shower and try to pretend it was like any other day.

A jolt ran through me. My heart skipped a beat. I had an idea. I stepped back to the secretary's desk and slid the top drawer out. My fingers ran over a collection of pens and pencils, pads of Post-it notes, and a pack of cigarettes. Huh. I wouldn't have guessed she was the type. There was a box of paper clips, and I stuck my finger in, saying a quick prayer. Bingo! There it was, a small silver key.

I pulled it out and fought the urge to dance around in circles with the key held above my head. I slid the key in and jiggled the lock a bit, and it popped right open. The file drawer slid out smoothly. My fingers ran over the folders. They had color-coded tabs on the top for each year. I found my folder and yanked it out. There was a slip of paper clipped to the front that held my dad's contact information and all sorts of "in case of emergency" details. There was a copy of my transcripts with all my grades. Four years at Evesham, and it amounted to little more than five or six sheets of paper. My passport was tucked into a pocket of the folder, and after a small shake it slid out into my hands.

I heard a shuffle outside the door. I froze in place, not even breathing. The steps moved down the hall, and my heart started to beat again. My eyes shot to the clock. It was time to get out of there. I shoved the passport into my bra and shut the cabinet drawer. I took a couple steps before I realized I had forgotten to lock the drawer. My fingers fumbled with the key and I dropped it onto the floor with a curse. Then the lock clicked and I slid the key back into the paper-clip box.

I put my ear to the door to see if I could hear anyone in the hallway. It was quiet. I pulled the door open a few inches and peeked out. No one. I stepped out into the hallway and headed toward the stairs. I'd only made it about three or four steps when I heard Dean Winston. He was talking to someone as he came up the stairs. Why did he have to pick that day of all days to choose to come into work early? My eyes darted around the hallway. There was a long wooden table against one wall, but there would be no way Winston would miss me crouching under there.

I ran past Winston's door and down the hall. At the very end of the hall there was a door that led to a second-floor balcony. I could hear Dean Winston getting closer. Any second he was going to turn the corner on the landing and see me. I hit the latch on the door, and it flew open, spilling me out onto the deck and into a pile of snow. I stood quickly and shut the door. The balcony had a picnic table and a few chairs sprinkled around. They were covered in snowdrifts. Near the door was a coffee can filled with sand and cigarette butts. This must have been where the administration staff came to take their smoke breaks. I waited to see if Winston had heard the door and would come to investigate, but after a minute it was clear no one was coming. All I had to do was wait a few minutes to be sure Winston was tucked away in his office, and then I could slip back into the hall and get out of the building.

I made myself count to sixty, five times. I bounced on the balls of my feet, trying to stay warm. I didn't want to move too close to the end of the balcony, in case anyone on the ground would look up and see me. When the time was up, I went to open the door, but the handle didn't budge. I let go of the handle. I refused to believe it was locked. I closed my eyes and took a deep breath. I took hold of the door and gave it another yank. It didn't even rattle in the frame. Then I saw it, a wooden block leaning up against the brick wall. The kind of block that would be handy to prop open a door that had an automatic fire door lock.

I was locked outside. I wanted to throw myself onto the balcony and have a meltdown, complete with screaming, kicking feet, and flailing fists. I'd managed to break into Winston's office and steal my passport, and now I wasn't going to be able to get away with it because I was stuck on the terrace. I'd either freeze to death or have to beat on the door until someone came to let me out, and with my luck it would be Winston. Even if it wasn't him, there was going to be a whole bunch of questions about what I was doing there.

I leaned against the door. My body was still humming with energy. I didn't want to give up. There was a tree near the corner of the balcony, its branches hanging over the railing. I walked over and looked down, and then back up at the branches. They were thick and sturdy, close to the balcony, and at least the thickness of my thigh.

People climb trees all the time. It is practically an American pastime. Baseball, apple pie, Boy Scouts, and climbing trees. Cats can climb trees, and they aren't even that smart. Statistics about how many people fall out of trees flashed into my brain, along with the odds of impaling myself on a branch if I fell, but I pushed these thoughts out of my head. Sometimes the payoff is worth the potential risks. My brain started going through the geometry, the angle of the branches, the distance to the ground. It looked easy. If I stood on the banister of the balcony, I would be able to reach one of the larger branches. Then just a few hand-over-hands and I would be near the tree trunk. It looked like I would be able to climb down, to the ground. It was basically a jungle gym with sap and bark.

I was going to have to make a decision soon. I needed to get off the balcony, pick up the duffel bag that I'd dropped outside my dorm window, and then get over the fence before too many people were up and around. Hopefully Drew would be around to give me a ride, but I had to leave time to walk to the airport, just in case.

I could do this. I would do this. I glanced down to make sure no one was walking through the quad below. I stepped up onto the brick banister that ran around the balcony. It hadn't looked that high up when I'd been standing next to it, but being an extra three feet up suddenly made it seem a lot higher. I wouldn't have been surprised to see a plane shoot past my ear. I reached up and grabbed the branch. I gave it a shake to make sure it wasn't rotted, before I let my weight hang on it. I also figured this would flush out any rabid squirrels. All I needed was some rodent chewing on my fingers. With the way this breakout plan was going, I wouldn't have been even remotely surprised if one did. The branch seemed stable, and no squirrels came rushing out in attack mode. I took another quick look down to make sure no one was around, and then when I saw it was clear, I took a step off the banister.

The branch held. My legs swung free and I decided not to look down again. My hands shuffled along the branch. I felt a splinter run into my pinky finger. I hummed the theme song that went with the army commercials and pictured myself in camo being all I could be. My hands shuffled a few more feet, and then my feet, found the branch beneath me. Almost there. I took a step onto the branch, bringing me closer to the trunk.

Then my foot slipped on an icy patch on the branch and slipped off. The sudden shift of weight put me way off balance. I felt my fingers slide on the branch above me. There was a beat when I convinced myself it would never happen, and then I fell. I felt the branches break beneath me as I plummeted toward the ground.

Then it went dark.

28

My eyes struggled to open. Everything hurt, even my eye-lashes. I stared up at a white ceiling. My mouth tasted funny, like I had been sucking on rusted nails. My tongue seemed to be stuck to the roof of my mouth. I couldn't tell where I was. I turned my head to the side. It felt as if the entire world slid off the axis and my stomach flopped over. I closed my eyes quickly, trying to get my sense of balance back. My eyes opened again, and I saw there was an IV pole. I followed the plastic tubing down from the pole to where it was connected to my arm.

IV. White. Hospital. I had to be in a hospital. Then the fall from the tree came rushing back to my memory. I'd fallen. There was a bright flash of pain in my leg. I glanced down. There was a giant cast that went from above my knee all the way down, with just my toes peeking out the end. Looked like the fall hadn't ended well.

"Hail?"

I turned my head slowly to the other side. Kelsie was sitting in a chair next to the bed. Her eyes were red and her face splotchy. She'd been crying.

"Can you hear me?" she asked, her voice shaking.

I tried to nod, but moving my head up and down made the sickening bed spins start again, so I stopped.

"Oh my god. I'm so glad you're awake." Kelsie grabbed my hand.

"Is there anything to drink?" I asked, my voice coming out raspy.

Kelsie leapt into action. She poured a glass of water from the pitcher on the rolling table next to the bed and jabbed the bendy straw into the glass. She held it out, and I took a sip. The cool water tasted better than anything I could imagine. I took another sip, but Kelsie pulled the glass away before I could finish.

"Careful. Not too much. Do you want me to get your dad? He's downstairs talking to one of the doctors."

"My dad's here?" My brain tried to find something to hold on to that made sense. I'd been trying to get my passport so I could see my dad in Chicago. What was he doing in Vermont?

"The hospital called him right away. He flew in last night. He's super-worried about you."

"Last night? How long have I been out?"

"A day. The doctors said it was a concussion. There have been a few other times when you seemed to come around, but you didn't make much sense. Mostly just mumbling and stuff."

"Huh." I closed my eyes. My stomach was starting to feel better. At least I didn't feel quite so much like I was going to throw up at any moment.

"Hail, you have to know I am *so* sorry. I have never been so sorry in my whole life." Kelsie started crying again.

I patted her hand absently while I searched my memory to figure out why she was sorry. Right. She'd been seeing Tristan. Maybe it was the fall, but I couldn't remember why it had made me so upset to start with. They would be good together. This could be what they meant by having sense knocked into you. Why had I been so concerned about the relationship with Tristan? I didn't love him. "It's okay," I mumbled.

"I never thought you would do something like this. I just feel sick," Kelsie sobbed.

"Something like what?"

Kelsie stopped crying for a beat and looked at me. "Suicide," she whispered.

I tried to sit up, and then froze when every muscle in my body screamed. "Suicide? I fell," I explained.

"Everyone is saying you tried to kill yourself when you heard about Tristan and me."

"If I'd wanted to kill myself, I would have jumped off the top of a building, not from the second floor." I couldn't decide if I was more offended that people thought I was the kind of person who would kill myself over a boyfriend or that I was apparently too stupid to know how to do it right.

"Ms. Sullivan gave a talk at the morning assembly and said your kind of attempt can be seen as a cry for help." She sniffed. "It's like when someone takes only a few pills or does superficial cutting."

Great. It sounded like Ms. Sullivan had finally found something to keep her busy. She was most likely giddy with all the excitement I'd caused. "It wasn't a cry for anything. I was trying to get out of the administration building," I tried to explain.

"Why didn't you use the door?"

"It's a long story." I could tell that she didn't believe me. She acted suddenly fascinated by a microscopic-size chip in her fingernail polish. "It was an accident, Kels."

"Then, why did you leave a suicide note?"

"What! I didn't leave a note." Then my mind flashed to the note I had meant to keep people from coming after me when I left for Chicago. I wanted to pull the covers up over my head.

"There was a note. I saw it; someone leaked to the Web already." She slapped her hand over her mouth. I guessed she wasn't supposed to upset me further by telling me that my latest adventure had also made the tabloids.

"Can I see your phone?" I said. Kelsie opened her mouth to protest, but I held my hand out. She passed me her phone, and I did a quick search on the Internet. The story popped right up on one of the celebrity sites. I skimmed past the headline and story and read the note again, to see if it sounded as bad as I'd feared.

Please don't worry about me. I have to go away. No one is making me do this. Please don't blame anyone. This is my decision. I know my leaving will upset people. I don't want anyone to be hurt or angry, but this is something I have to do. Please try to understand.

I closed my eyes. It sounded worse than I'd imagined. I might as well have ended the note by writing GOOD-BYE, CRUEL WORLD! and drawing a skull or a black heart.

"It'll be okay." Kelsie patted my arm like it was a kitten.

"I jumped off the balcony because I didn't want to get caught for having broken into Winston's office. I needed my passport for identification for the plane, so I took it out of his secretary's file cabinet. My plan was to go to Chicago to see my dad. We had another fight and I wanted to see him."

"We thought you had your passport on you so your body could be identified."

"I was jumping from the second story, not into a farm combine. I would have been identifiable."

"Unless you landed on your face," Kelsie pointed out.

Our eyes met, and we started to giggle. "Good point. Never land on the face."

"Well, I suppose the silver lining is that you don't have to travel to Chicago. Your dad's here. Not to mention you don't have to take a cheap discount airline. If you're going to travel, go first class, or don't bother going."

"Whew. Saved from the horrors of low-cost coach travel. All I had to do was break my leg and knock myself out." I laughed again.

"I am sorry about Tristan, you know," Kelsie said. "I was going to tell you a thousand different times, but then I never could bring myself to do it. At first I excused it by telling myself nothing was happening. We were just flirting, joking around. Then when it was more, I didn't know how to stop."

"Do you love him?" I asked.

Kelsie's eyes filled back up with tears. "I know I shouldn't, but I think I always have."

"It's okay. You'll be good for him. He always needed someone who would keep him more on his toes."

"He still cares for you."

"I care for him, too. I never stopped. We were good together, just not meant to be a couple forever. I think both of us stayed because we loved how comfortable it felt. Stability is a good thing, but not everything."

"You still must have been mad that I didn't tell you. You shouldn't have heard it from someone else."

"I wasn't exactly making myself easy to talk to," I admitted.

"You pulled away from everyone. Not just Tristan, everyone. It was like you put yourself in exile. It was like you didn't want to be our friend anymore."

"I know. At first I was sure it was everyone else, but I think you're right. I did exile myself. Maybe I needed the space to figure things out, figure me out."

"Did you?"

"Nope." We laughed. "But I'm making headway. At least I'm doing something about it instead of waiting for someone else to figure it out for me. I'm not sure where life is going to take me, especially when Dean Winston figures out I broke into his office and wasn't suicidal. But at least now I feel like I'm going somewhere," I said.

"Can I come with you?" Kelsie's voice was serious.

"Can't imagine going anywhere without my best friend," I said.

Kelsie threw her arms around me. "As long as you know that if I'm going, we're going first class."

29

After Kelsie left, I closed my eyes, and I must have fallen asleep, because when I opened them again, the room was dimmer, the late afternoon light turning silver gray. I saw a figure standing in the doorway, but with the bright light from the hall, I couldn't make out who it was.

"Dad?" I asked.

"He just left. He went down to the cafeteria to get something to eat. Watching you sleep can wear a man out." Drew stepped into the room.

"I was just dozing." I ran my fingers through my hair, trying to make it look decent, or at least not horrid. I wiped my tongue over my teeth. They felt a bit furry. No one had brushed them for me while I was out cold. My breath probably smelled like dirty gym socks.

"Dozing, huh? You always snore like a truck driver when you doze?"

"I wasn't snoring," I insisted.

"Oh, I'm sorry. You weren't snoring. You were simply choking to death on a live ferret."

I pressed my lips together to keep from laughing. Drew pulled the chair closer to the bed and sat. Great. He was close enough now to see the smell waves coming out of my mouth.

"Just so you know, typically, bungee jumping works best when you wear the bungee part." Drew motioned to my leg. "How are you feeling?"

"A bit rough. You know what they say. The fall went fine right up until the very end." I picked at a loose thread on the blanket. "About the last time we were together . . ."

"You want to apologize."

I met his eyes, surprised he knew what I was going to say.

"The thought of not having a chance to kiss me again made you throw yourself off a roof. I should be more careful. I know the effect I can have on women."

I threw one of my pillows at him, then winced from the effort. He caught it before it even came close to his face.

"I was going to apologize for hitting you. There was no excuse for that. And I didn't throw myself off the roof—for you or anyone else." I had the feeling I was going to be explaining this to people over and over for weeks. I paused, trying to find the words to explain to Drew how I felt. I couldn't explain it to myself, so I wasn't sure how to tell him.

"I know you didn't try to kill yourself. You're crazy, but not that kind of crazy. Besides, now that you've seen the glory of Denny's, you've got too much to live for."

"The stuffed French toast was pretty amazing."

Drew poured a glass of water. "I brought you some more ice while you were out." He held the glass so I could have a drink. "I figured you'd be thirsty. I've been knocked out a few times in hockey. I always wanted a giant glass of water when I came around."

"Thanks. It was nice you came."

"I keep telling you, I'm a nice guy." Drew looked around to make sure we were still alone. "In addition to checking on you, I came to tell you something."

"Sounds very top secret."

"I know who's leaking all the stories to the tabloids."

I sat up, ignoring the flash of pain. "Who?"

"Mandy Gallaway."

My mouth fell open. "Why would she sell stories to the press? She hates the tabloids. And it's not like she needs the money."

"You might be wrong about that. I asked around. Turns out her grandfather controls the purse strings and he thinks some of her shenanigans make the family look tacky. Sounds like he's limiting her allowance. Now, she still is getting more money than the average family of four, but with her tastes she's going to need any extra coin she can get her hands on."

"Did you actually just use the term 'shenanigans'? Are you channeling your inner eighty-year-old?"

"I think you're focusing on the wrong thing again."

"Are you sure that it's her?"

"I'm sure. She's ticked off a lot of people on staff. It's one thing if she wants to do her own thing, but letting that security guard take the heat was low. The guard was put on unpaid suspension for two weeks. The maid who cleans her room saw the leaked photo of Mandy on her laptop and did some poking around. Mandy's doing it under a fake name, of course, but she's definitely the leak."

"Should we tell the police?" I asked. I enjoyed the image of the cops coming and taking Mandy down, maybe handcuffing her in the middle of the morning assembly, or perhaps they could set the police dogs loose on her.

"Selling out your friends isn't a crime, just disgusting. The police aren't going to do anything."

"She's not my friend."

Drew leaned back. "That's true."

"What should I do, then?"

"Up to you, but if she blames anything else on the staff, I'm going to make sure it comes out." Drew shuffled his feet. "I should go, let you get some sleep."

"No," I said quickly. "I mean, I'm not tired. You could hang out if you want."

Drew smiled. "Looks like the only thing you needed to enjoy my company was a hit on the head."

"That's not true." I could feel my face flushing.

"It's okay. I'm teasing you. Don't worry about what happened before. I was the one out of line. I shouldn't have kissed you like that. We'll just pretend it never happened. Friends?"

I opened my mouth to tell him I didn't want to be his friend. What I wanted was for him to kiss me again. Preferably when I was out of the hospital and had a shower.

"Hey, there."

Both Drew and I whirled to face the door. My dad was standing there, holding a take-out container of Baskin-Robbins ice cream. I was willing to bet it was mint chocolate chip, my favorite. As he came into the room I saw he hadn't shaved, and his shirt was missing a button.

Drew stood up. "Hello, Mr. Kendrick. She's awake now. I think her snoring finally woke even her up."

My dad smiled.

"I wasn't snoring," I repeated.

Drew and my dad shook hands, ignoring my protests.

"Thanks for keeping an eye on her while I ran out. Would you like some ice cream?" My dad asked Drew, holding up the bag. I hoped he had another flavor in there, because I wasn't planning on sharing my pint.

"I should be going. Besides, I'm sure you'll want a chance to catch up." Drew grabbed his jacket by the door.

There was still a lot I wanted to talk about with Drew, but I didn't want to have that conversation in front of my dad. If I hadn't been hooked to an IV, with my leg in plaster, I would have followed Drew out into the hall.

"See you soon?" I asked, hoping I didn't sound too needy.

"I'm like gum under a desk," Drew said. "Next to impossible to get rid of."

30

My dad bustled around finding spoons and bowls for the ice cream, making the entire process seem more complicated than pulling together an entire Thanksgiving dinner for a family of twenty. He was constantly in motion, a blur in the room. A blur who kept avoiding my eyes. The entire time he was getting things ready, he kept up a nonstop stream of chatter. He told me about how the airline had lost his luggage and he'd had to buy a sweatshirt from the hospital gift shop, and how the ice-cream store had been out of butter pecan, so it wasn't really thirty-one flavors, only thirty.

"Dad?" I didn't say anything else until he finally stopped moving and looked at me. "I wasn't trying to kill myself."

His face turned gray, and his eyes shifted away. "Of course not. I never thought that."

I could see he had thought it, that he was still thinking it. "I was upset about our conversation," I said, trying to explain what had happened.

My dad turned back to dishing out the ice cream. "We don't need to talk about that now. I thought maybe when they spring you from here we could take a small vacation. Maybe go someplace warm."

"I don't want to go on vacation."

"If this is about Linda, then you don't need to worry, she won't be coming." He passed me a wad of napkins. "She and I are going to take a break."

"You broke up with her?" Great. Not only was I ruining my own love life, but now I had managed to ruin my dad's, too. "I didn't want that."

My dad patted my leg. "It's nothing you need to worry about. All you need to focus on is getting better. A vacation will do us both some good."

"I can't go on vacation. I've got school." I could feel my frustration growing.

"You let me take care of school. I'll talk to your teachers and we'll work something out. They can give you some projects to work on long-distance."

"I don't want you to take care of it." My hands were balled into fists at my side.

His face fell. I could see he was hurt. "Okay. If you don't want to go anyplace, we don't have to." He stared at his bowl of ice cream, then perked up with a smile. "Heck, you're right.

Who wants to deal with airlines and traveler's tummy? We could go up to your grandparents'. We can rent a bunch of movies and hunker down, maybe play some board games. Remember how you used to kick my butt at Monopoly? I bet if we ask nice, we can even get your grandma to make her famous spaghetti and meatballs."

"I don't want to go to grandma's, either. What I want is for you to listen to me! For once don't try to solve the problem or shove it out of the way. Just listen!" I yelled.

My dad went silent, his face still for the first time. A nurse peeked in to see what the fuss was about, but backed out when she saw my dad. "I listen to you, Hailey," he said.

"No, you don't. You hear what you want to hear, or you end any conversation you don't find comfortable."

He rubbed the palms of his hands on his pants. "I should have told you about Linda. I realize now how wrong I was about that. I didn't want you to think I was being disrespectful to your mom."

I flopped back down onto the pillow. "This isn't about Linda. And it isn't about Mom, either. It's about us."

"What about us?"

"Just that. There is no us anymore. I don't even know if you like me."

My dad grabbed my hand. "Of course I like you. I love you. I love you more than anything else in my life."

"Then, why is it you never want to be around me? First it was school, but then it was all the time. You're always too busy.

There's always a good reason why you have to run off. Then you changed our summer plans. You say you love me, but you don't even know me anymore."

"That's not true, Hailey." He ran his hands through his hair. "I get distracted with work, but I've never taken my focus off of you."

"Really? What's my favorite subject?"

"You like science." He looked relieved, as if I had asked him an easy question.

"It's history. I act like it's science because you like science. I figured it would give us something to talk about. I'm not even sure I want to major in it anymore."

"But you get straight A's in science." He sounded confused.

"I don't care!" I used my ice-cream spoon to point at the door. "Who was the guy that was here?"

"Drew?" My dad looked at the door as if he were hoping Drew would reappear and provide some answers. "I assume he's one of your friends from school. Isn't he the one dating your friend Kelsie?"

"Kelsie is dating my boyfriend, Tristan. Drew works the janitorial crew at Evesham."

"A janitor?"

I could see my dad's brain spinning, trying to figure out why a school janitor had shown up at the hospital to visit me. "Remember how Dean Winston assigned me to a cleaning crew as part of my punishment? That's how I met Drew. He's going to Yale."

His eyebrows drew together as he tried to sort out what direction the conversation was going in. "He got a janitor job at Yale?"

"No. He got accepted there," I said. "He's going to major in English."

"Oh. That's good."

"I think I like him."

My dad nodded very seriously. "That's good too. He seems like a very nice young man."

"Except I blew it. He kissed me and I slapped him, and now he doesn't want to be with me. All he wants is to be friends." I grabbed my dad's hand before he could say anything. "Please don't tell me how you don't know what to tell me and that mom is the one who would have handled this kind of boy-girl stuff. Mom is gone. I wish she wasn't, but she is. You're the only parent I've got left."

My dad got up and moved so he could sit on the bed next to me. He had tears in his eyes. "I'm sorry, Hailey. I let you down. I let your mom down. If she could see what a mess I've made of things, she'd be so disappointed."

"I think she'd be pretty ticked at me, too," I said.

"We'd both be grounded."

"Remember how when she was really mad she would give herself a time-out?" I said.

My dad laughed. "She used to crawl back into bed with a book. She said life would be better if everyone took a time-out when they needed one."

"I miss her." My eyes spilled over. With all the crying I'd been doing lately, I was going to have to increase my water intake or run the risk of dehydration.

"I miss her too. She was a hell of a woman. You remind me of her."

I wiped my eyes. "How?"

"Your mom was persistent. She used to say it didn't matter if she won the race but that she kept going even when she fell down. She wasn't a quitter. That was one of the reasons I was crazy about her. I was always worried about what other people thought of me. I didn't ever want to look stupid. Your mom didn't worry so much about other people. She kept her focus on not letting herself down. I can tell you've got that same focus. You're going to go far. She'd be the first person cheering you on."

I smiled. I had a memory of her being at one of my school recitals in elementary school. She'd been the only parent giving a standing ovation. Maybe that's how you know someone loves you; they make you want to be a better person by believing in your effort, not just your accomplishments.

My dad handed me my bowl of ice cream. "Okay, let's get back to the issue. If you like Drew, why did you hit him when he kissed you? Was it that bad of a kiss?"

I laughed. My leg was broken, I had a concussion, and I was most likely in the largest amount of trouble I'd ever been in at school, and suddenly it felt like things had never been better.

31

I shifted in the wheelchair. I had wanted to walk out on my crutches, but the hospital had some sort of policy against it. You would think they would want people to walk out. It would make it look like people got better in the hospital, but no. I was parked in the lobby waiting for my ride.

I'd sent my dad home yesterday. He'd offered to be the one to take me back to school, but I knew he needed to get back to work. The past three days we'd talked like we hadn't in years. We'd made plans for spring break. We were going to go down to North Carolina, just the two of us, but on the way back my dad was going to arrange for me to meet Linda. He'd offered to cancel his summer plans in London, but suddenly it didn't seem as important as it had earlier. We'd talked about how London was full of history and maybe I'd spend at least part of my summer with him over there. I didn't know what else I would do with my summer, but I was okay with that.

Finally the car pulled up to the hospital doorway. The nurse who was pushing my chair through the doors let out a gasp when she saw who it was. She was so focused on him, there was the very real chance she would have let me roll into oncoming traffic.

Tristan opened the passenger door of his car. "Your chariot awaits," he said, bending low.

"My chariot is late," I pointed out.

"Not just late, fashionably late." Tristan put his hand on my back as I crutched my way into his car. "Watch the ice. You don't want to end up back in there five minutes after getting out."

Tristan turned on his charm for the nurse as he gathered up my bags and took the discharge papers. If she asked him for an autograph, I was going to push her down with one of my crutches. He climbed in and waved to the crowd that was gathering near the door. I was starting to feel like we were in a parade. Tristan jacked up the heat in the car before taking off. We drove in silence out of town toward school.

"Thanks for picking me up," I said.

"What are friends for?" Tristan glanced over and smiled. "Kelsie wanted to come too, but Dean Winston wouldn't let both of us leave campus. She's looking forward to seeing you. I should warn you, I think she's planning some sort of welcome back party."

"I'm not sure Winston's going to approve a party." My dad had met with Dean Winston after my accident. I was still on restriction for the next three months, and I'd been moved to working in the library so I could still help pay for the statue as long as I was in a cast, but everyone else was off restriction. My dad had hinted that Dean Winston's actions had been designed to ostracize me and no doubt had led to the amount of stress I was under. Winston was probably worried that we would sue him for emotional distress that resulted in me throwing myself off the administration building. My dad had clarified that I'd been after my passport and not trying to do myself in, but clearly my decision-making had been impacted by all the stress. I was willing to bet Dean Winston couldn't wait for spring to come and for me to graduate. However, he had decided to allow me back at school, and there wasn't going to be anything on my permanent record either.

"It won't be a wild party. No strippers or Jell-O wrestling. More of a friends-welcoming-a-friend-home party. How can he have a problem with that? If it makes you feel better, we can say the party is a going away party for Mandy." He glanced over quickly to see my reaction.

"She's leaving?"

"She may have already left. She wasn't around this morning. The official story is that she wants to move back to New York to be closer to her half sister."

"I didn't think she spoke to her sister."

Tristan shrugged. "I'm not sure she's even met her half sister before. Her mom has been married more often than most people change their underwear. I don't think anyone buys the story, but if it makes her feel better about things, it's no skin off my nose."

In the hospital I'd debated how to handle the Mandy situation. Drew had been right; it wasn't illegal, so the police wouldn't care. I could have turned her in to Dean Winston, but I wasn't interested in helping Winston out in any way. I could have confronted her myself, but ending up in a catfight with her didn't seem like a good plan. She struck me as the kind who would fight dirty. She was probably a hair puller. Then I'd end up with a bald spot in addition to the cast on my leg.

In the end I went to the person who had the most experience with the tabloids, Tristan. He'd come to the hospital, and we'd had a chance to talk. Being able to focus on the situation with Mandy let us get over what was between us. Seeing him reminded me how much I liked him. I didn't love him, but I did want him in my life. If he was going to be dating my best friend, there had to be a way for us to be friends.

Tristan and I discussed the idea of leaking our own story to the tabloids that would out what Mandy had done. The public would eat up the idea that she was so desperate for attention that she'd placed her own stories in the news. I could picture the headline PAY ATTENTION TO ME! in a giant font smeared across a picture of Mandy running from a pack of photographers. While that was an appealing image, I didn't like stooping to her level, and Tristan wasn't keen to help the tabloids sell any magazines.

In the end Tristan met with Mandy. He let her know we

knew what she had done, and if a single story about anyone on campus came out, we would make sure stories about her flooded the press, and they wouldn't be stories she wanted. Tristan said that she had started off by crying, but had ended up yelling that everyone was jealous of her fame and then storming out. When he'd told me that, I'd felt sick. I'd hoped the whole situation would be resolved, but it seemed like Mandy might make things worse.

What neither Mandy or I had counted on was the reaction of everyone else at Evesham. The night after Tristan met with Mandy, we filled in Kelsie and Joel, and word started to spread that Mandy was the leak. People stopped speaking to her. They shunned her. Tristan said it was like people thought she had leprosy or a really nasty STD. Apparently it was all too much for her. I shouldn't have been surprised. Mandy didn't mind if people liked her or loathed her, but she couldn't stand to be ignored.

"There's something else I should tell you before we get back to school," Tristan said. "Joel and I talked last night."

"Oh? What about?" I fidgeted in the seat, avoiding Tristan's eyes. The last thing I needed to do was spill my guts, only to discover they had been talking about baseball statistics.

"He told me what happened that night, that he was the one you were kissing."

So much for hoping it had been a random sports discussion. "I can explain . . ."

"You don't need to explain. Joel told me he was the one

who kissed you and that you kept it a secret to protect him. He would have lost his scholarship if you'd told. Not that any of that excuses the fact that he's my best friend and he kissed my girl and then lied to me about it."

"Are you mad at him?"

"We're guys. I punched him, he hit me back, and then everything was fine. We went out for ice cream after."

I rolled my eyes. Men.

"I can't blame the guy for wanting to kiss you," Tristan said.

"I never wanted you to get hurt," I said.

"I know." Tristan paused, chewing on his lower lip. "If you guys want to go out, date or whatever, that would be okay with me."

I touched his shoulder. "I like Joel. He's always been one of my closest friends, but that almost works against us. It's almost too comfortable. There's no spark." I shrugged. I didn't know how to explain it. Logically Joel would make a great boyfriend, but sometimes the heart isn't logical. "I don't think he and I are meant to be, but I still appreciate you saying it."

"Feel good to be back?" Tristan asked as we pulled through the school gates.

I watched the line of trees that lined the driveway march past until we came into the quad. I looked up at the library, the gray stones covered in ivy. To my left were the dorm buildings. From the outside I could spot the windows for my different rooms over the years. I realized how well I knew this place. I knew how the second sink on the right in the bathroom never had really hot water. I knew the best place to sit in the library, and how the toffee chocolate chip cookies in the cafeteria were worth every calorie. I knew which stairs creaked and how if you wanted extra towels, you could bribe the maids by bringing them Starbucks from town. I hadn't wanted to go to Evesham, but in its own way it had become home.

"I can't believe I'm going to say this, but I think I'll miss this place after graduation."

"You know what they say: Loyalty, Duty, and Honor."

"That saying used to drive me nuts."

"I guessed that, after you went all whack job on the Tin Man."

I shoved Tristan in the shoulder. "I feel bad about that now. I think I was missing the whole point. It's not about blind loyalty and doing what you're told. It's about being loyal to yourself and those you respect, and about doing what you have to do, even when you're afraid."

"For graduation maybe all of us should get tattoos with the logo on it." Tristan pointed to his bicep. "Right here. That way we'll never forget our time at Evesham."

"Or each other."

"I got to tell you, you're not the kind of person that is easy to forget. Besides, we're all going to stay in touch. There isn't going to be a chance to forget."

32

We were late. The morning assembly had already begun. The drama teacher was at the lectern talking about a field trip to New York to see some productions. Parents would have to pay the costs, but those who went and wrote a paper had a chance to earn some extra art credits. Dean Winston's eyes narrowed when he saw Tristan and me slip in the back. It was hard to be subtle, since I was on crutches. Tiptoeing in wasn't an option. Then there was the fact that Kelsie was waving at us like we'd been separated for years instead of a couple of days. She slid over on the bench to make room for me. Tristan made sure I made it safely to the row, and he made a funny face at Kelsie. She started giggling. At this point everyone was looking at us; even the drama teacher had stopped talking. From the back I could see the vein in Winston's forehead starting to throb.

I sat down as fast as I could and let my cast stretch out into the aisle. Joel had saved Tristan a seat a few rows ahead on the guys' side. Joel turned around and smiled. He mouthed the words "Welcome back" before turning back around.

The drama teacher picked up where she'd left off. The school would book rooms at the Library Hotel for three nights. I could hear a few people whispering. Weekends in New York were always popular. I wondered if the drama teacher believed that everyone who signed up was really interested in the plays. She must have thought Evesham was full of theater geeks.

Dean Winston got up as soon as she sat down. "For those of you considering the trip, be aware you'll be expected to sign the code of conduct agreement before you go. This means you will be held to the expectations of an Evesham student." His eyes swept the room as if he could tell already that people were planning to sneak out of the hotel and try to get into the clubs. "Evesham students should always demonstrate the highest standards of quality."

Kelsie poked me in the side with her elbow, and I pressed my mouth down to avoid giggling. I went to poke her back and accidentally hit my crutch, which fell into the aisle with a loud clang. Kelsie snorted, and I bit my lip to stop smiling.

Dean Winston stopped mid-word and froze me in place with his stare. "Is there something you find funny about this, Ms. Kendrick?"

Everyone turned around to look at me. "No, sir." I made a vague gesture with my hand to the crutch. "It just fell."

"Ms. Kendrick, will you please step forward?"

"Oh, shit," Kelsie whispered under her breath.

I picked up my fallen crutch and went up the aisle until I was standing just in front of the lectern.

"This school is founded on principles, Ms. Kendrick."

"Yes, sir." I could feel everyone's eyes on me. My face was burning hot.

"You've been doing some research on the history of the school, haven't you?"

"Yes, sir."

"Then, perhaps you'd like to share with the group what you've learned thus far about the principles that are the cornerstones of this institution?"

The last thing I wanted to do was share, but I had the sense that he wasn't really asking it as a question. He twirled his finger, indicating that I should turn around to face the audience.

I turned to face everyone and cleared my throat. "Evesham is named after one of the two main battles in thirteenth-century England. It was part of the Barons' War. The school's founder, Simon Kenilworth, started the school in 1911 with the idea that it would provide an opportunity for privileged young men to complete their education, with a focus on also developing their character. He'd attended boarding school in England and felt that there should be a school of equal caliber here in the United States. The school started admitting girls in the 1960s."

"Thank God," someone in the crowd said. Winston searched

the crowd to see if he could tell where the comment had come from.

"And do you believe in the principles this school was founded upon?" Winston asked me.

"Yes and no," I answered honestly.

Winston's nostrils flared in annoyance.

"I've come to realize that the school is only a collection of buildings. History teaches us that nothing is permanent, but I do believe in this place, if by 'school' you mean the people who have gone here."

"If this school is so important to you, Ms. Kendrick, perhaps now you would be willing to share the name of who you were with the night you destroyed the statue that represents the principles you say you hold so dear."

I opened my mouth to tell him again that I wasn't going to tell. Not now, not even if he dragged me up in front of a million assemblies.

"I was the one with her," a voice called out.

I looked up. Drew was standing in the back. He walked down the center of the aisle until he was standing by my side.

"I was with Hailey that night. It was my idea to destroy the statue," he said.

"I hope you realize this means you're fired," Dean Winston said.

"What are you doing?" I whispered to Drew.

"It doesn't matter that I wasn't there. I wish I had been,"

Drew whispered back. He smiled, and I felt my heart turn over. "I'd choose to be with you anytime, anywhere." He squeezed my hand, and we turned to face Winston together.

"It wasn't him. I was the one with Hailey!" Joel yelled out.

Joel was standing up. I could tell he wanted to throw up, he was so scared, but he was standing up for me.

"Actually, it was me," Kelsie called out, and she stood as well. She gave me a thumbs-up.

"Nope, it was me," Tristan said as he stood.

I felt my eyes start to fill up. There were squeaks and rustles as more and more people started to stand in the hall.

"It was me."

"I was there."

"I was with Hailey."

"I did it."

Soon more than half of the student body was standing up. Everyone from my old crowd was standing, and even a bunch of people that I didn't know that well.

Dean Winston looked like he was ready to have a stroke. His entire head had gone red, and the vein in his forehead was thumping like it was laying down a club beat.

"Everyone return to their seats. Right now," he yelled. He pointed at me. "Return to your place, Ms. Kendrick."

Drew walked by my side until I got back to my seat. I smiled at everyone as I walked past. They might have been mad at me, but they'd never abandoned me. If it wouldn't have gotten me into more trouble, I would have stopped to hug each and every person as I went by.

"You can leave now," Dean Winston directed Drew.

Drew winked at me. "I'll catch up with you later." He walked out of the assembly with his head held high. A few people, many of them girls, turned to watch him leave.

"Oh, now, he's dreamy," Kelsie whispered. "You should hang on to him."

"I plan to," I whispered back.

33

Winston ended the assembly just a few minutes later. He was deflated like a helium balloon the morning after a birthday party. There was a sense in the room that things had changed. Or maybe it just felt that way to me.

Instead of running to class when the assembly was over, almost everyone stopped to tell me how glad they were to see me back. Tristan had his arm draped over Kelsie's shoulders, and she was busy inviting everyone to the party she was planning.

"Oh! Maybe we should do costumes! We could make it a theme party, dress up like your favorite past Evesham student," Kelsie said, her eyes sparkling. "Or people could just pick a time period they like, anytime since the school started." She never met an event that wasn't made better by dressing up.

"I bet my parents could snag some great 1920s costumes," Tristan suggested.

"I love those flapper outfits!" Kelsie squealed. A few of the girls surrounding us started to buzz with ideas for food and decorations. It was rapidly changing from a small welcome back party to an A-list event.

Joel touched my elbow softly. "I'm sorry," he said, so quietly that only I could hear him.

"Me too."

"I should have owned up to Tristan long ago. I never should have left you hanging. I didn't exactly come across as a real knight in shining armor."

"You stood up for me when it mattered. And you told Tristan when you didn't have to. Besides, I think, since I tried to behead one, I'm not all that keen on shining armor types anyway."

"Even without the armor, I'm guessing there isn't going to be a you and me, is there?" Joel asked.

I shook my head. "Someone's going to be lucky to get you, though."

We hugged. "There will always be room for you to visit at the White House," Joel said.

"Visit? What happened to my ambassadorship?"

Joel snapped his fingers. "Right, I almost forgot. You wanted someplace like the Arctic, right?"

I pleaded that I had to go, leaving everyone else to plan the party. It was going to take me time to get across campus to class with my crutches, and I wanted to go back to my room first to pick up my things. Kelsie offered to come with me, but I waved her off. When I stepped outside, the sun was shining. There were still splotches of snow around, but there were also shoots of green popping up from the mud. Spring was coming.

I'd hoped Drew would still be around, but I didn't see him anywhere. I started heading toward the dorms. A horn beeped, and I turned to see Drew sitting in his truck parked in the lot. I smiled and headed over. He got out to meet me halfway.

"You've got some nice friends there, Prima Donna."

"I do."

"I'm glad things are working out."

"Yeah, about that. Some things haven't worked out." I took a deep breath and reminded myself, no guts, no glory. "I need to tell you something. I don't want to be friends with you."

Drew blinked. "Sort of wish you had said something before I opened my big mouth to Winston and lost my job."

This wasn't going the way I'd expected. I tried to figure out how to explain everything. That I liked him. I wanted to be with him. I'd only slapped him because I hadn't been expecting the kiss. I'd been confused, but I wasn't confused anymore. I knew what I wanted. My brain scrambled for the words that would make all of this make sense and leave Drew with no choice but to throw his arms around me, but I couldn't think of a thing.

I dropped one crutch and grabbed Drew by the shirt and yanked him close and kissed him. The entire world shrunk down to the point where our mouths met. I felt off balance, and not just because I had only one good leg. The air outside was cool, but I wasn't remotely cold. I felt like my entire body was thawing out. The kiss lasted forever, but eventually we both pulled back. Drew was quiet.

"Aren't you going to say anything?" I asked. He remained silent, so I kept going before I could lose my nerve. "I like you. I was afraid to say anything, but something you told me stuck with me. How being brave is about being scared but doing it anyway. That's why I kissed you. You may not want to be with me anymore, and I can understand that. I'm high maintenance, and it apparently takes me a long time to sort out what I want. Sometimes I come across as stuck-up, but it's more because I only know my own world. I'm bad about trying new things unless someone pushes me. I'm a lousy cleaner."

Drew put his finger over my mouth. "You also talk too much." He leaned in and kissed me again. He pulled back and cupped my face in his hand. "It also took you long enough to figure this out."

"You're saying you knew I liked you?"

"Oh, yeah. Written all over your face. I figured you just needed to get to the answer on your own."

"Is that right?"

"Yep. You were crazy about me from the start. You needed some shaking up, and I was just the guy to do it."

"You got me. As soon as I saw your prowess with the floor buffer, I was yours."

"Chicks dig men with mechanical skills. Evolutionary."

I rolled my eyes. "I'll have you know I don't need anyone to buff my floors."

"Very true. That's one of the things I like about you." Drew smiled. "I always went for the independent type. That, and I find plaid skirts and knee-highs hot."

The bell tower chimed the hour. A few Evesham students started to rush for class.

"I have to go."

"I know. You better buckle down. If I'm going to show you all the dive bars that offer karaoke around Yale, you're going to have to do your part and keep your grades up so you get in."

I took a few steps toward the dorm, but then turned back. Drew was still standing by the truck. It reminded me of how my mom would always wait to make sure I got inside safe when she dropped me off someplace. An idea came into my head.

"Hey!" I called out to him. "You want to come to a party later? My friends are throwing a thing, and I want you to meet them."

"Sure. Count me in."

"By the way, you're going to have to wear a costume."

Drew's eyebrows pulled together. "Dress up? Like what? I don't know—"

"What's the matter? Are you afraid?" I held my arms out, using my crutches to wave around the quad. "You gotta live life, suck the marrow from its bones!"

Drew laughed. I headed back toward the dorms. It was going to be a busy day, and I didn't want to miss a moment of it.

I didn't plan to miss another moment of the rest of my life.

ACKNOWLEDGMENTS

A writer without a reader is a lonely thing, so the first thank-you goes to you for reading this book. With so many good books and not nearly enough time to read them all, I appreciate your taking the time with mine. I want to say a particular thank-you to two of my teen readers, Valentina Misas and Abi Coale. Not only did they read my books and write to tell me they liked them, they spread the word to all their friends on Facebook and in school hallways. I couldn't ask for a better promotion team. I think you guys are awesome. To everyone else who wrote to tell me they liked my books—thanks. You made my day, sometimes the entire week.

I am so fortunate to have a great team behind each of my books. My agent, Rachel Vater, picked me out of the slush pile and has cheered me on since. The entire team at Simon Pulse is fantastic. Thanks to Cara Petrus (cover design goddess), Annette Pollert, Anna McKean, Amy Jacobson, and Emilia Rhodes. Special thanks to my editor, Anica Mrose Rissi, who is not only an editorial genius, but shares my love of shoes and dogs. Thanks for all your guidance, insight, and willingness to put up with me and my tendency to use Canadian spelling and stick *u*'s into every other word. I hope I can write books with this team for years to come.

My friends and family continue to support my dream of being a writer and are just darn fun to have around. Big thanks to Avita Sharma, Shannon Smith, Jamie Hillegonds, Serena Robar, Alison Pritchard, Laura Sullivan, Shanna Mahin, Joelle Anthony, Brooke Chapman, Joanne Levy, Carol Mason, Robyn Harding, Lynn Crymble, Jeanette Caul, and Melissa Mills.

I couldn't do any of this without my husband, Bob, who not only provides technical support, cooks meals as needed, and is never jealous of my legions of imaginary friends, but can also always make me laugh. This journey wouldn't be nearly as much fun without you. To my dogs, stop chewing my shoes.

ABOUT THE AUTHOR

EILEEN COOK spent most of her teen years wishing she were someone else or somewhere else, which is great training for a writer. When she was unable to find any job postings for world-famous author, she went to Michigan State University and became a counselor so she could at least afford her book-buying habit. But real people have real problems, so she returned to writing because she likes having the ability to control the ending. Which is much harder with humans.

You can read more about Eileen, her books, and the things that strike her as funny at eileencook.com. Eileen lives in Vancouver with her husband and dogs, and no longer wishes to be anyone or anywhere else.